Tales From
The 7,000 Isles

Popular Philippine Folktales

Tales From
The 7,000 Isles

Popular Philippine Folktales

Retold by
Art R. Guillermo, Ph.D., and
Nimfa M. Rodeheaver, Ph.D.

Illustrated by Tina Sevilla

Read Me Books A Division of Vision Books International

Library of Congress Catalog Card No. 95-60276

International Standard Book No. 1-56550-030-X

Library of Congress Cataloging-in-Publication Data:
  Guillermo, Art, Ph.D.,
  Rodeheaver, Nimfa M., Ph.D.
  1. Juvenile fiction 2. Philippines, The I. Title
    Library of Congress Catalog Card No. 95-60276
  ISBN 1-56550-031-8

Cover art: Tina Sevilla
Illustrations: Tina Sevilla
Cover design: Nadise Whiteside
Design and typography: Nadise Whiteside and Christina Vaughan
Editor: Christina Vaughan

Printed in the United States of America

Read Me Books
Vision Books International
3360 Coffey Lane
Santa Rosa, CA 95403
(800) 377-3431
FAX (707) 542-1004

*This book is dedicated
to our wonderful
children and grandchildren,
who light up our lives with blazing
warmth and serene hope.*

CONTENTS

ACKNOWLEDGEMENTS

We owe a debt of gratitude to the following people who helped immeasurably in the preparation of this book:

- Al Barrios, for the pronunciation key to the Pilipino words in the text.

- Margaret Bacigalupi, for the artwork critique.

- H. Victor Rodeheaver, for reading and editing the original manuscripts.

- Beatrice Shepard and Claudia Kelsey, for providing the secondary source of the folktales.

- Corazon B. Guillermo, for her delightful critique of the stories.

- Tina Sevilla, for the fascinating illustrations of this book.

INTRODUCTION

The Philippines is a land steeped in fairytales, legends, and myths. Before Ferdinand Magellan claimed to have discovered the land in 1521, the islands, which were ruled by sultans and datus, were already flourishing with their own written language, literature, and folk stories. Christened for Spain's King Philip II, the Philippine Islands were colonized for some 380 years. The colonizers tried to suppress native cultural traditions and expressions, but the people discreetly carried on their folk epics in oral forms.

When the Americans came in 1899, they started the public school system. People were now encouraged to write down their stories, legends, and myths. Oral folklore was painstakingly put down in writing by dedicated Filipino and American scholars to bring this hidden treasure of rich literature to light for people's enjoyment.

As the Philippines recovered from the devastation of World War II, a cultural renaissance arose and swept the country, bringing out the best in art, music, and other cultural expressions. Traditional Philippine legends are being told in new and fascinating ways.

Storytelling is a universal form of entertainment. To the Filipinos, it is a traditional practice. In the splendor of telling stories, they subconsciously passed on to their children and grandchildren cultural traits, wisdom, morals, and practical lessons. Children are always fascinated when they gather around lolo (grandpa) or lola (grandma) to listen to tales of heroic characters, mythical monsters, and legendary places. During those magic moments, their imaginations are kindled by a world of fantasy and mirth.

There are hundreds of folktales of the Filipino people. Every language group and every ethnic tribe has its own unique and fascinating tales. Not surprisingly, many of these tales have a common thread and theme, so it was quite difficult for us to choose which stories to include in this book. After much consideration, we chose tales which are common to the major ethnic tribes. Also, because of the frequent occurrence of the same character in many different stories, we made our choices to reflect a variety of characters in this collection.

This book provides a fresh approach to these legendary tales from the 7,000 Isles. We have taken the liberty of introducing embellishments and fanciful scenarios to make each tale more dramatic.

A pronunciation key is included at the bottom of each page in which unfamiliar words occur to provide readers a perspective of the cultural setting of the stories.

We hope our readers will enjoy this collection of the best of Philippine folktales.

The Authors

MAP OF THE PHILIPPINES

SOUTH CHINA SEA

PACIFIC OCEAN

• Laoag

MOUNTAIN PROVINCE

Cagayan River

• Bontoc

Lingayen Gulf

• Baguio

LUZON

Angeles

• Cabanatuan City

Malolos

• Quezon City

Olongapo

• Manila

The Philippines

Bataan

Cavite

MINDORO

• Legaspi

SAMAR

PANAY

LEYTE

Iloilo •

LEYTE GULF

NEGROS

• Cebu City

BOHOL

Mactan Island

CEBU

Dumaguete City

PALAWAN

MINDANAO SEA

SULU SEA

• Marawi City

MINDANAO

Zamboanga

Midsayap

MORO GULF

• Davao

SULU ARCHIPELAGO

CELEBES SEA

THE PHILIPPINES

The Philippines is an archipelago of over 7,000 beautiful islands–depending on whether it is high or low tide. Fewer than 500 islands are larger than one square mile. The country has a total land area of 115,700 square miles. Luzon is the largest island, where the majority of the population live. Because the archipelago is situated in the tropical zone, the country has only two seasons–wet (rainy) and dry (summer). The land is rich with natural resources. Its lowlands are heavily cultivated for rice, the staple food of the people.

The country has a population of 68 million. Metropolitan Manila, the capital, is the largest city, with a population of 8 million. The people speak many languages and dialects, but the lingua francas are English, Pilipino, and Spanish. English is used in schools, universities, government, and mass media. Private and public education are available to the people. Besides having one of the highest literacy rates in Southeast Asia, the Philippines claims to have the freest press in that region of the world.

Philippine flora and fauna are distinctive in their tremendous diversity. Abundant rain and sunshine produce an incredible variety of plant life, such as the giant narra tree and the legendary bamboo tree, of which there are 54 varieties. There are thousands of varieties of flowers which give the country their beauty. Two of the more spectacular flowering plants are the *waling-waling,* whose flower measures 12.5 centimeters across, and the National Flower, *sampaguita,* which is fragrant and star shaped.

Animal life is remarkable for the absence of predators. The country's largest wild animal is the rare tamaraw, a variety of water buffalo, which figures in one of our stories in this book. The Philippine eagle, the world's second largest (after the South American harpy eagle) survives precariously in its habitat on Mindanao. Marine life is rich with its 2,400 species of fish. Sports fish, such as swordfish, sailfish, and marlin, are found in abundance. The world's smallest fish–7 millimeters long–the translucent dwarf pygmy goby, is found in rivers near Manila.

Besides its natural beauty and bountiful resources, the Philippines is known as the crossroads of East and West, which has enriched the lives of the Filipino people. From the Spanish they received their religious orientation, from the Americans they obtained their democratic and educational institutions, and from the Chinese they inherited their mercantile acumen. These influences produced the ilustrados, mestizos, and technocrats which make Philippine life and society an interesting mixture of ancient ways and modern possibilities.

Origin of the 7,000 Isles

In the beginning, Bathala,[1] the Great Spirit, created only the earth, sea, and sky. There were no stars, no sun, no moon.

One day the earth was in turmoil. There was a rivalry between the sea and sky. Violent winds raged across the empty space. The sea was shooting mountainous waves at the sky. In turn, the sky was raining down enormous rocks at the sea.

Witnessing this as he sat on his golden throne in the heavens, Bathala, the Creator, was angry with the chaotic world. He decided to set things in order.

Bathala commanded them, "Stop fighting and settle your differences!" The stormy sea and the unruly sky obeyed the Great Spirit. Peace reigned on the surface of the earth.

Scattered all over the azure sea were the rocks showered by the sky. They turned into thousands of beautiful islands. With gentle waves and balmy breezes, the sea caressed the islands. This is how the 7,000 pearly isles of the Orient seas were born.

Silence and darkness still enveloped the earth. In the heart of silence, the islands were shrouded in misty blackness. There was no light, only darkness.

"There must be light to show the land," Bathala said.

He took a clod of soil, molded it into a gigantic ball and flung it across the sky. The ball stayed up in the sky and it became the sun to shed light on earth at daytime. Then he molded a smaller ball and flung it also across the sky. It hung just below the sun and it became the moon. Night and day appeared on the earth.

Bathala wanted to give beauty to the sky, so he gathered thousands of stones and threw them into the far reaches of the heavens. These

---

[1]Bathala - Baht `HAH lah. Supreme Spirit and Creator

became the brilliant stars, the twinkling lights that shone at night. Darkness disappeared on earth.

The sky was beautiful, but the earth was still barren, lifeless. Bathala took his magic wand and swept it across the land. Many kinds of trees and plants sprang to life. Flowers bloomed in profusion in fields, valleys, and on the mountains. The islands were ablaze with colors of the rainbow. The vast blue sky was filled with white, fluffy clouds.

Then the Creator said, "It's a beautiful world down there. I will create human beings in my own likeness to enjoy the beauty and goodness of the earth."

He sent his messenger Lawin[2] to look at his creation. Lawin flew over thousands of islands. Soon his mighty wings grew weary. He circled above the forest and finally rested on a bamboo tree. It was quiet—very quiet.

Suddenly Lawin heard a thumping noise and a shrill cry, "Who-o-sh! Who-o-sh!" It was coming from the node of the tree. Then he heard a voice pleading: "Please let me out. I want to be free."

Lawin quickly cracked open the node with his powerful beak. Out came Malakas,[3] a handsome, brown-skinned lad. Thus the first man appeared on earth.

Another voice was heard from another node of a bamboo tree. The voice was also pleading to be free.

Lawin lost no time in cracking the node, and another human being stepped forth. This was Maganda,[4] a comely maiden with dark brown eyes and flowing jet-black hair. Thus the first woman appeared on earth.

In time, Malakas and Maganda fell in love with each other and Bathala married the loving couple.

Soon the couple had a child. Then many more children were born to Malakas and Maganda. This is the origin of mankind and the creation of the beautiful islands where they lived happily ever after.

---

[2]Lawin. `LAH-oo-een. Messenger of Bathala, eagle
[3]Malakas. Mah Lah `KAHS. First man on earth
[4] Maganda. Mah Gahn `DAH. First woman on earth

Why the Sea is Salty

A long, long time ago, the sea was fresh and clean. People drank pure, clear water from the sea. Fish life abounded in the crystal waters surrounding the island of Palawan.

Living on the big island was a tall and handsome man named Kanag.[1] Among his people he was the apo,[2] the wisest and the strongest. Being born of a Diwata[3] and a mortal man, he had the strength of a hundred water buffalos. With his strength, this kindly chief cut down trees from the forest to build homes for his people.

Kanag was an orphan and, when he grew up, he lived alone in his sprawling home of bamboo and lauan[4] on the mountain top of Magat. There, nights were cold and haunted by the singing of mourning doves.

In his loneliness, he visited the seashore to enjoy the cooling sea breeze. As he stood on the shore, he turned his sharp eyes to gaze across the sea. He spied another island. Jutting out of the island was a peak on which stood a maiden who was waving as if she were in distress.

Kanag leaped quickly into the sea. As he waded across the water, his footprints left deep caverns on the ocean floor which became shelters for thousands of brightly colored fish.

When the maiden saw him crossing the sea, she rushed to the shore to meet him. Upon seeing her, Kanag was immediately smitten with love. The beauty of this woman was far beyond the beauty of any of the women in his village.

Kanag asked why she beckoned to him as if she was in distress. The maiden replied, "I'm Princess Napintas[5] of the island of Purok. I've heard

---

[1]Kanag. `KAH Nahg
[2]apo. `AH Poo. Chief
[3]Diwata. Dee `OO-ah Tah. Goddess
[4]lauan. Lah `OO-anh. Hardwood tree
[5]Princess Napintas. Nah `PEEN Tahs

of your strength from my people. Since then I've been climbing up that peak in hopes of getting your attention because I need your help."

Kanag was curious about what kind of help she would need from him.

Napintas told him of a dream which haunted her every night. It concerned a dream house, which her father the Datu[6] was unable to build because he had been killed during a battle. Now it was her responsibility to finish her dream house.

She described the house of her dreams. "It must be located on the east side on a lofty peak of Purok where the house will be bright and sunny in the morning. The house must be constructed of bricks as white as the feathers of banatiran,[7] the whitest of mountain doves."

Kanag was challenged by these plans for an unusual house. He was undaunted, for he knew that with his ability he could do the job. He replied, "Napintas, your request for my help in building your dream house is indeed challenging. Inasmuch as I'm a lonely man, I long for a wife. Will you be my beloved wife when I finish building your dream house?"

With a whimsical smile, Napintas demurely nodded her head in agreement.

Kanag immediately departed for his own island, leaping with giant steps over the waves. More underwater caverns were created by his immense footprints. The ocean creatures were very happy because the deep crevices made more shelters for them.

Napintas' request for a white house caused him to wonder. How could he build a house made of white bricks? Where would he get the white clay to make bricks? Aha! Suddenly he remembered the cave in the mountains where his people obtained the white sand called asin.[8] His people used asin as flavoring for their food and as a means of preserving fish, deer and boar meat.

Kanag found the cave, dug out the asin and molded it into salt bricks. After he had an ample supply of bricks for the house, his next task was to transport the salt bricks to the island of Purok. He then constructed a bridge with spans of bamboo and posts of lauan. The bridge stretched

---

[6]Datu. `DAH too
[7]banatiran. Bahn ah `TEE RAHN. Mountain dove
[8]asin. Ah `SEEN. Salt

for hundreds of miles across the open sea.

Kanag happily employed thousands of his people to carry the salt bricks across the bamboo bridge. His people were also happy, for they knew that their chief would soon have a wife.

The work of ferrying the salt bricks went on for many moons. With the heavy loads being carried day and night, the bridge soon began to sag and sway. Displeased by the noise of the carriers as they tramped across the bridge, the ocean sent monstrous waves which beat against the bridge supports.

With a thunderous roar, the bamboo bridge collapsed. The crash was heard as far as the distant islands. Tons and tons of salt bricks fell into the bottom of the ocean. The salt bricks melted quickly in the fresh water and spread rapidly throughout the ocean.

Standing on her lofty peak, Napintas saw the terrible catastrophe and was stricken with sorrow. Tears cascaded profusely from her eyes and flowed down the mountainside to mingle with the salty waters.

And so it is today that the sea is salty.

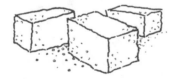

Coconut
The Tree of Life

In the beginning of the world, the Great Spirit and Creator Bathala covered the land with all kinds of living things. Trees and other plants flourished over the face of the earth. The land was filled with many-colored sweet-scented flowers.

Although the emerald green surface was a pleasant sight, the arrangement was in disarray. Tall and sturdy trees, short and skinny trees, bushy and graceful shrubs and plants stood side by side. Scrawny weeds and stubby fruit trees carpeted the hills and valleys.

All trees and plants had the ability to walk and talk. They could live wherever they wished. However, each tree or plant spoke only to their own kind. They failed to understand the language of their neighbors, causing much confusion.

Bathala was not pleased with the situation. "Each family of trees should live in harmony with the others," he said. He wanted plant life to grow with pride and dignity.

One day, Bathala called all the trees and other plants to a summit meeting at the Great Hall in the sky. He ordered each family to send a representative.

There was arguing among the trees and other plants as to who could best represent them, but finally the selections were made. The trees voted to send Narra[1] to represent all hardwoods and evergreens. Cawayan[2] was hailed as the spokestree for grasses and weeds. The fruit trees chose Manga[3] to speak for the fruit bearing trees. Palay[4] was picked to speak for all grains and root crops. Niyog[5] was the choice of all the tallest plants and

---

[1]Narra. Nah`RAH. Mahogany tree
[2]Cawayan. Kah `OO ah-ee ahn. Bamboo tree
[3]Manga. `MAHN Gah. Mango tree
[4]Palay. `PAH Lah-ee. Rice plant
[5]Niyog. Nee `EE-ohg. Coconut tree

all the nut-bearing trees.

At the Great Hall, Bathala presided over the summit meeting. He ordered that each representative be given a chance to state briefly the qualities of his or her family in order to provide him with the facts on which to base his decision. He told the trees that he wanted an orderly arrangement of tree and plant life on the surface of the earth.

The first to plead his case was the proud Narra. "I'm Narra, the biggest, tallest, and strongest of all trees. My over-arching branches and sky-reaching leaves are home for Lawin and all the big birds. People use my sturdy trunk for the posts of their houses. Where I grow, the deer seek shelter under my shade. I am called the King of Trees."

Praising Narra, Bathala said, "Well said, Narra. You may step aside." His audience shook their branches to show their appreciation.

Next to speak was the graceful Cawayan. "I'm the tallest and largest of the grass families. I have the right to choose wherever I want to live because I'm needed by the farmers. They weave mats out of me for the floors and walls of their houses. My skin is woven into dainty baskets and also made into fish traps. I'm useful as a fence on the farm to keep out alingo.[6] Farmers call me the Mighty Grass."

Bathala said. "Good job, Cawayan. I'm pleased to hear of your usefulness. You may step aside."

Next was the gorgeous Manga. She addressed Bathala with grace. "I'm Manga, the leader of all fruit trees and I produce the best of all fruits on earth. We keep people healthy with our rich and nutritious fruit. My mangos are very sweet and delicious. When they ripen, they send out their sweet smell. My juice is sought for its tarty sweetness, and my pulp is preserved for dessert. People call me the Queen of Fruits."

Bathala was delighted with Manga's qualities.

The next presenters were the representatives of the smaller plants. It was Palay's turn to speak for all the edible grains and root crops. Willowy Palay stood up and told Bathala, "I'm Palay, the many-splendored grain. People eat me at every meal. I provide energy to people and help them live longer. Cakes made from my glutinous kernels are the most delicious desserts. Farmers love to plant me because I grow fast. They enjoy reaping my golden stalks. Celebrations are held for me after a plentiful harvest.

---

[6]alingo. Ah`LEEN goh. Wild pig

I'm known as the Grain of Life."

"Thank you, Palay, for your contribution to the lives of all the people. You may step aside," Bathala said.

The last to speak was stately Niyog. He came prepared with a brilliant speech.

"Bathala, thank you for creating me as I am. You have given me a bountiful body, luscious fruit, and useful leaves. Everything I have is useful to people. I'm their shelter and their food. I've the sweetest juice, which people love to drink at their parties. I've milk which makes savory cakes. My white meat is made into oil. Fiber from my husk is made into ropes and woven into mats. My shells are used for cooking food. I bear plenty of nuts in all seasons. Whenever my fruit is harvested, I grow more. I am deeply rooted, so typhoons cannot break me. My fronds are woven for shade from the hot sun. People call me the Tree of Life."

Bathala was impressed. "Indeed, you are wonderful, Niyog!"

When all the delegates had spoken, Bathala told the trees that from here on, their ability to move and to talk would be taken away so that each family could be settled in a suitable place. And so Bathala declared his decision to issue an order for plant and tree life on the surface of the earth.

He assigned all evergreen trees to mountain tops in the far northern parts of the earth, where it is cold and misty, to let them grow stalwart and hardy.

The hardwoods were given the eastern side of mountains, just below the evergreens, where there are rains and lots of sunshine to toughen their trunks.

Fruit trees were located in the lowlands where there is plenty of moisture to enable them to produce luscious fruits.

Grain plants and root crops were sent to the lowlands where they could be nourished by the flowing river waters, so they can grow energy-laden golden kernels.

Coconuts, the trees of life, were awarded the backyards of homes, orchard groves, and mountain slopes, where people can easily obtain them for their many uses.

And that is how the Supreme Creator Bathala set his greenhouse in order. The decision made the trees and plants happy. The summit of trees and plants was a great success. So it is today that trees and plants have their own places to live in happy harmony on the surface of the earth.

Legend of
Fruits and Vegetables

When the world was young, there were only two people — Lakan and Kislap — who lived on the island of Mindanao. This was a long, long time ago.

They were created from clay by Minaden,[1] the supreme god, who shaped the clay into human form. Then he told the wind god to breathe the breath of life into them. Minaden married them, but for a long time they were childless. They kept praying to Minaden to give them a child.

The goddess Diwata was sent to visit the couple. When they saw Diwata, the couple asked about their prayers.

"Have you heard our prayers, Goddess Diwata?"

Diwata eagerly responded, "Your prayers have been heard. Minaden will grant your wish." With her magic wand, she touched Lakan and Kislap and left for the sky world.

In due time, Kislap brought forth a man child, a strapping lad who became the center of their lives.

One of the gods in the sky world was furious that Minaden had given Lakan and Kislap a man child. He was Meketefu,[2] brother and co-creator of Minaden. He had the power of life and death on the entire island. He was mean and evil. When Minaden decided to answer the couple's prayers, Meketefu was not consulted. He had wanted a female child instead, so, when the man child was born, he vowed to make the life of Lakan and Kislap miserable.

He cast his spells and sent strong winds and rain to flood the plains and hurled thunder and lightning to frighten the man child. Then he called off the rain and caused a terrible drought. The rivers and lakes dried up. Fish died. Forest trees shriveled. Birds disappeared. Deer also died

[1]Minaden. Mee`NAH Dehn. Supreme God and Creator
[2]Meketefu. Meh Key `TEE FOO

because there were no young leaves to feed on. Famine stalked the land. Meketefu reveled in the misery which he had caused on the island and to its first inhabitants.

The famine in the land had already taken its toll on the first family. There was nothing to eat. No meat was found which would have made them strong. Soon the man child grew weak and died. The couple were heartbroken and wept bitterly over the loss of their son.

Minaden saw what was happening to his creation. He was very angry with what his brother had done. He summoned Meketefu to appear before his throne.

"You have done a terrible thing to my creation, Meketefu. Now I command you to cease all these terrible deeds. We must do something to comfort Lakan and Kislap, and keep alive the memory of the man child. Do you have any suggestions?"

Meketefu smiled. "Yes, sir. My suggestion is that we change the remains of the man child into plants which will bear edible fruits."

Unhesitatingly, Minaden sent Meketefu to console the grieving couple Lakan and Kislap.

Meketefu told them, "Weep no more, my children. Our Supreme God Minaden has sent me to tell you that your loss will bear many good things in the future."

He then ordered the couple to bury the remains of the man child in a clean plot behind their bamboo hut, and to keep the plot clear of weeds.

One wonderful sunny day, strange plants started to sprout all over the plot. Lakan and Kislap were filled with joy upon seeing the variety of plants which were starting to grow. In time, the various plants bore fruits of many sizes and colors. Colorful fruits were seen, such as emerald green, golden beige, purple, orange, yellow, and many more. Some were hanging from branches and some were found under the soil.

Meketefu returned to visit the happy couple who didn't know what to do with the various fruits produced by the plants.

"These are the good things that were promised to you. The fruits of these plants are good to eat. Some you should harvest when they are ripe, others when they are fresh and tender," he said. He pointed out the ripe fruits and the fresh tender ones.

The fruits looked like the different parts of the human body. Meketefu named the various fruits.

One kind of fruit looked like the head which Meketefu called taro.[3] The arms and fingers became saging,[4] the fingernails became buyo,[5] the teeth became maize,[6] the bones became cassava,[7] the umbilical cord became palay,[8] the eyes became duhat,[9] the brains became lime, the ears became the betel leaf, the limbs became sugar cane, and the intestines became sweet potatoes.

Meketefu told them to keep the seeds of each fruit so that they could plant them all over the island.

One plant that the god pointed out to the couple was the rice plant, with shiny white edible kernels. "Take good care of this plant, for it came from the umbilical cord of the man child. Planting the seeds of rice every rainy season and harvesting the yellow grains will provide you your staple food for the rest of the year. Rice will also make you live longer on this earth," Meketefu told the grateful couple before he returned to the sky world.

At last, Lakan and Kislap had many things to remind them of their first son. Their harvest filled their bamboo hut. They had plenty of fruits and grains to eat. In time, they raised many healthy children who populated the big island of Mindanao.

To this day, rice has been the staple food of the inhabitants of Mindanao and the other islands of the Philippines. That is how the edible fruits and vegetables came to be.

---

[3]taro. `TAH Roh. A root crop
[4]saging. `SAH Geen. Banana
[5]buyo. `BOO Yoh. Areca nut
[6]maize. Mah `EES. Corn
[7]cassava. Kah `SAH vah. A root crop
[8]palay. `PAH Lah-ee. Rice plant
[9]duhat. Doo`HAHT. Berries

Golden Boy

In a mountain village on the island of Panay there lived a couple named Ka Doro and Ka Pura. Their hut was surrounded by a garden planted with many kinds of vegetables. They sold their produce every weekend in the village market.

One special vegetable they grew best was upo.[1] Upo is a climbing vine with wavy tendrils which entwine on bamboo trellises. Upo sold by the couple was the sweetest in the village, and was the envy of their fellow farmers. Their produce commanded a higher price at the market.

One day, they discovered that their upo plant had no new blossoms. There were none of the yellow flowers that usually covered the branches in wild profusion. They were alarmed at the loss of their prize money-maker. They stopped going to their market stall. Their customers missed their favorite gourd.

Saddened at the loss of their most popular produce, Ka Pura turned her head to the sky world and prayed to Bathala, "Great Bathala, Creator of the World, hear our prayer. All these years, we have prayed for a son or daughter. Our prayers have not been answered. Now our upo plant which has been giving us food and money is not producing any more fruit. We pray that you will make our upo plant flower again," Ka Pura pleaded.

One sunny morning as usual, Ka Pura was out watering the barren upo vine. She peered through the thick tangle of vines and saw a tiny yellow flower growing from the tip of a branch.

"Naku Po!"[2] exclaimed Ka Pura, greatly excited at seeing the evidence of a new fruit. Her shouts of surprise brought Ka Doro running to her side.

"At last, Bathala has heard our prayers," Ka Pura said as she looked up to the sky world with clasped hands.

---

[1]upo. Ooh `POH. Gourd
[2]Naku Po. Nah Koo `POH. An idiomatic expression of surprise "Oh my Lord!"

They watched every day as the little yellow flower gradually turned into a tiny ball with a cute tiny tassel. The ball grew into a big green upo. Its skin had pretty lines which looked like ribbons tied around the fruit. They could hardly wait to pluck it from the vine.

Harvest time came. They plucked the big upo. It took the two of them to haul the gigantic fruit to the kitchen. Indeed, this was the biggest upo they had ever grown. They were not going to sell it. They were going to make a meal out of it.

Ka Pura grabbed her bolo[3] to slice into the upo when she heard a tiny cry come out of the fruit: "Please don't hurt me! Please don't hurt me!"

Ka Pura screamed "Naku Po!" as if she had heard a multo.[4] Ka Doro came running to her side and asked what all the screaming was about. She pointed to the upo and told him about the squeaky voice that sounded like an infant.

Taking the bolo from here, Ka Doro gently and very carefully sliced open the upo. Out popped the most beautiful baby boy they had ever seen. The baby was already standing up and had curly brown hair like the silken tassel of new corn, and milk-white skin.

Before their astonished eyes, the sweet lad smiled and softly said, "Bathala heard your prayers. I'm the son you have prayed for, and I was sent to you through this upo. I have come to live with you."

The couple shouted with great joy and lovingly welcomed their precious baby boy. Their barren life was now enriched by the presence of this new human life.

"We will call you Mahal,[5] because you are loved," said Ka Pura to their infant son.

Ka Pura immediately prepared to bathe Mahal. She raced to a spring and filled her bucket with pure fresh water, while Ka Doro brought in a large, tightly woven bamboo basket to use as a bathtub.

Using a coconut shell, Ka Pura scooped water and poured it tenderly on the baby's head. The water cascaded over the child's body. Then, when the water hit the bottom of the tub, they heard a metallic jingle like

---

[3]bolo. `BOH Loh. Long knife
[4]multo. Mool `TOH. Ghost
[5]mahal. Mah `HAHL. Love

the sound of many coins piling up. They saw a pile of gold nuggets at the foot of the baby.

The couple were astonished. Mahal was smiling broadly, and told Ka Pura to pour more water over him. Ka Doro gathered the nuggets, which filled a sack.

Now they felt that they were indeed rich beyond their dreams.

While Ka Pura held Mahal, she suggested that they should build a mansion to replace their small nipa hut. Ka Doro added that their lot was too small for a mansion.

Ka Doro said, "We should have a ten-hectare lot for this mansion."

They continued to make plans while Mahal sat in silence in a corner. He was quietly put aside while the couple argued about the number of rooms, size of the kitchen and servant quarters.

Their thoughts became more ambitious. They also talked about a cottage in the mountains where they could escape from the summer heat.

Looking at their sack of nuggets, they decided that it was not enough to buy all of what they needed, so Ka Pura went out to the spring to fetch a bucket of water. They wanted more gold nuggets.

When Ka Pura poured the water over the baby's head, Mahal jumped out of the bamboo basket and looked at the couple with a big frown on his face. Then Mahal, in a loud voice, said as he pointed his little finger at them, "What greedy parents you turned out to be. You were not happy with one sack of gold. You wanted more. Since you can't be content with what I brought you, I am going back to Bathala. I shall take this gold back with me. Goodbye."

The sweet little boy became smaller and smaller until he had shrunk and vanished from their sight. Ka Doro and Ka Pura were ashamed and cried in self-pity because of their greed.

Well, they were back to raising vegetables. No more upo plant. And they were as poor as before.

Monkey Prince

Once there lived on the island of Maran a dashing prince. He was gentle and kind to his people, who adored him as the future sultan. Every lovely girl in the kingdom wanted him for a husband. The sultan's attempts to find the prince a suitable wife always ended miserably.

Prince Rajan was much too enthralled with his cherished pastime. He liked to hunt alone with his bow and arrow and his dog Dugo. The game he hunted was usually the slick white-tail deer or the white-tusked black boar that roamed the deep forest.

Often, Rajan was out hunting for days. The Sultan and Sultana were gravely worried because they had heard about a wicked witch who lived in a dark cave in the deep forest. She was Dayang, who could take the form of an animal or human being. She enjoyed luring lost hunters to her cave where she changed them into pigs.

Rajan was not worried about being lost. His friends the birds and the monkeys were always around to guide him along the right trails. His feathered friends also led him to where his prey could be found. Rajan had learned to understand the twitter of birds and the grunts of monkeys.

Dayang had her eye on the dashing prince. She had watched the kingly youth from behind the trees. She had developed a strong desire to have him as her husband, so she prepared a clever plan to catch the prince.

"I shall turn myself into a beautiful maiden, and appear on Lake Paway," she schemed.

Prince Rajan and his dog often stopped by the lake to quench their thirst and rest while hunting deer.

One sunny day, Dayang, dressed in a fetching sarong, was at the lake in the form of a beautiful maiden. Her skin glistened with perfumed coconut oil. She waited under a swaying coconut tree by the shore.

In a short while, an exhausted prince and tired dog appeared. They went straightway to the water to slake their parched throats.

When Prince Rajan turned around, he saw the beautiful maiden under the swaying coconut tree. In all his hunting days he had never seen such beauty.

He approached the maiden with great surprise. He introduced himself, and then inquired politely, "It is a pleasure to see you here, for I have not seen such a beautiful maiden in all my life. May I know who you are and what brought you here?"

"I'm Bugan and I come here often to fish. I live yonder, behind that grove of coconut palms. I would be happy to have you meet my parents, and perhaps serve you our fresh coconut milk," was Dayang's response to the unsuspecting and innocent Prince Rajan.

Since the prince and the dog were tired of hunting, the invitation was welcomed.

As they proceeded in the direction of Bugan's (Dayang's) house, Rajan's feathered and furry friends were in an uproar. They knew that Dayang was disguised as Bugan and of her evil ways of turning hunters into swine.

The birds led by Kalaw[1] were fluttering around him, warning him not to go with Bugan, but Prince Rajan paid no attention to them. The monkeys were swinging high up in the trees and screaming warnings about the disguised Dayang who would turn him into a swine. But Rajan paid no heed, for he had fallen in love with the beautiful Bugan.

On the way, the two rested beneath a leafy acacia tree.[2] As she sat beside him, she related stories about her life. Her eyes looked strange. They were like smoldering embers. They were mesmerizing him. Soon the eyelids of Rajan became heavy with oncoming slumber. At the moment when Rajan was about to fall into deep slumber, his monkey friends let out a piercing shriek which jolted the prince back to wakefulness.

Rajan came to his senses, and found that this beautiful girl Bugan was not the lovely one she seemed to be, but rather a witch in disguise, as his monkey friends had warned. He broke away from her side and bolted with his dog Dugo in a quick getaway. They ran like deer being chased by

---

[1]kalaw. `KAH Lah-oh. Hornbill bird
[2]acacia tree. Ah `KAH See-ah. Also known as monkey pod tree

22

a pack of hungry hounds. Kalaw and his monkey friends helped the Prince and his dog escape safely from the angry Dayang.

She resented the rejection and vowed to avenge her humiliation, so she planned another trap for the dashing prince. This time she would turn herself into a magnificent big-antlered stag.

One bright hunting day, Rajan and his dog spotted the stag prancing warily through the woods. Rajan thought that the antlers would make a fine trophy in the palace hall.

When Dugo caught the scent of the stag, the pursuit was on. Like a whirlwind, the stag raced through the woods in an attempt to shake off its pursuers. As they were about to close in, they saw the stag enter a cave.

When Rajan approached the cave, a stringy-haired hag met him. It was the evil witch Dayang. She was covered with a black cape. Shrieking bats poured out of the cave. Rajan was horrified. He wanted to run but his legs felt like stones.

Filled with rage, Dayang screeched at him and, instead of turning Rajan into a pig as she had done with her other victims, she pronounced a curse upon him.

"When you, Rajan, left me under the acacia tree and fled with your monkey friends, I suffered great humiliation. Therefore, you shall go with them and be a monkey. Your people of Maran will live also like monkeys."

On bended knee, he begged for the witch's forgiveness for the hurt he had done, but his pleas fell on deaf ears. She went on with her curse. "You shall be called the Monkey Prince. You and your people will only regain your human forms when another human being shows kindness and does a good deed for you."

Rajan became a big silver-backed gray monkey. His people turned into gray monkeys and made their homes in acacia trees. The whole island of Maran became known as the village of gray monkeys with a big silver-backed one—the Monkey Prince—as their leader.

In time, neighboring islanders liked to visit Maran—the Monkey Island—and watch the gentle simians feed on green bananas and golden mangoes thrown at them.

One day, a bunch of roughnecks from another island came to Monkey Island and tormented the creatures with sticks and stones. They had a devilish time taunting the Monkey Prince who looked so noble with his flowing silver mane. The Monkey Prince was bruised and bleeding from the abuse.

The roughnecks would have killed the Monkey Prince had not a visiting princess come to his rescue. Princess Vida took the wounded Monkey Prince to her home, where the palace shaman attended to his injuries by rubbing herbal medicine on the wounds. The Monkey Prince quickly recovered.

Before the astonished eyes of Princess Vida and her father, the big gray silver-backed monkey was transformed into a human being once again. A handsome man suddenly appeared before them. He was dressed in the clothes of a prince.

The man was Prince Rajan. The witch's curse was finally broken by the kindness of the princess. The monkeys on Maran also returned to their human forms.

When Prince Rajan took over as the Sultan of Maran, he chose the lovely Princess Vida to be his bride. In time, they had a dozen children who made them very happy. The new sultan gave up his favorite pastime to give more time to his people whom he served wisely and well.

Buffalo and Turtle

Once upon a time, the island of Marina was inhabited only by animals of many kinds. There were cats, dogs, turtles, rabbits, herons, hawks, eagles, and monkeys. There were also pigs, horses, cows, and the tamaraw.[1] All of them lived peacefully together, for there was plenty of food for everyone.

Each animal minded its own family. Each day was spent in the joyful tasks of eating, playing, and sleeping. Life on the island of Marina was peaceful but uneventful.

One day Pawikan[2] was out early in the field looking for the tasty kangkong[3] leaves. Tamaraw was out early, too, and was already munching on juicy ledda,[4] his favorite food.

While Tamaraw was searching for other clumps of ledda, he nearly stepped on Pawikan, who was so small that he was hidden by the thick clumps of ledda.

"Pardon me, Mr. Pawikan," Tamaraw apologized for the near mishap. "I didn't mean to step on you. This ledda grass is so thick that I did not see you."

"Oh, that's perfectly all right, Mr. Tamaraw. You didn't hurt me at all," said Pawikan. He was in a cheerful mood that morning.

"I'll tell you something. Why don't we play a game?" Pawikan quipped.

Tamaraw was rather surprised. He had never been invited to play in a game before. The other animals had hardly talked to him. Perhaps they were intimidated by his huge black horns and mean looking eyes. Tamaraw was a gentle creature at heart, and longed for companionship.

---

[1]Tamaraw. `TAHMah Rah-oo. Wild buffalo
[2]Pawikan. Pah `OO-ee Kahn. Turtle
[3]kankong. Kang KONG. Creeping vine with succulent stems
[4]ledda. `LEE dah. Grass

"Oh, what kind of game would that be?" asked Tamaraw. He was amused that a little bitty animal would ask him to play a game.

"Why don't you and I run a race? We'll begin here in this field and race to yonder mountain and back. Whoever returns first will be crowned the king of the fields," Pawikan explained.

Pawikan's suggested race raised the hackles of Tamaraw. The boldness of Pawikan to challenge him to a contest of speed and power was absurd, he thought. He belittled the idea. "Are you serious, Mr. Pawikan? Can't you clearly see how big and strong I am? Why, one leap of mine will take you a hundred leaps. You know who the winner will be," Tamaraw said disdainfully, as he leisurely grazed and chomped blades of ledda.

Pawikan was visibly stung by the haughtiness of Tam-araw, but he held his tongue and calmly pursued his proposal for the race.

"Well, if that is the way you feel, I'll tell all the animals that you are afraid to run a race with me," Pawikan taunted.

Tamaraw's ears perked up. Of course, he didn't want the other animals to think he was afraid to run a race with Pawikan, nor to give the impression that he was a loser. That would be just too much.

"Okay, then, Mr. Pawikan, we shall run a race and be done with it, but don't you dare tell the other animals that I was afraid of running a race with you." Tamaraw grudgingly admitted.

"Okay, that is what we will do tomorrow, Mr. Tamaraw," said Pawikan.

They started the race at sunrise the following day. The boundaries were established from the field of ledda grass to yonder mountains and back. Whoever came in ahead of the other would be crowned the King of the Fields.

Meanwhile, Pawikan called on his relatives for help. He told them that winning the race would mean a great boost to the dignity of all Pawikans. Most importantly, by winning the race, Pawikans would no longer be taken for granted.

He explained what they were to do to help him win the race. At every rest station along the way, a Pawikan would be stationed. There were twelve stations. When Tamaraw stopped to rest, a Pawikan would pop up and yell, "I'm here!" His relatives heartily agreed with the scheme.

All the animals were at the starting line and were anxiously waiting to see who would win the race. The odds were heavily in favor of Tamaraw, who was the biggest, strongest, and fastest animal on the island. There was no doubt who would win the race, but many of them secretly hoped that Pawikan, the underdog, would win.

Onggoy[5] was chosen referee. He alerted the racers to be ready in their positions. "Ready, get set, GO!" yelled Onggoy.

With a mighty heave, Pawikan got off as best he could with short legs and a shell on his back. Tamaraw shot off like a typhoon and was out of sight in a minute. He wanted to get the race finished early and teach the upstart Pawikan a lesson in speed.

At the first station, Tamaraw slowed down and headed to the cool shade of a coconut tree. He was confident that Pawikan was way, way behind. After all, his one leap would take a hundred leaps of Pawikan's effort.

Before Tamaraw could catch his breath under the coconut tree, he heard a Pawikan yell, "I'm here!" He couldn't believe his ears. How could that pipsqueak Pawikan get here so fast? he wondered.

However, Tamaraw was not discouraged. There were more stations up ahead where he could catch his breath, so he raced like an enraged bull to get to the next station. At every rest station, there was that pesky Pawikan, who mockingly yelled, "I'm here!"

Tamaraw was now completely demoralized. Near the finish line, he was panting for dear life. In fact, he was limping badly and he could see that Pawikan was already far ahead of him. All the animals were cheering for Pawikan, who was just a few yards from the finish line.

"Come on, Pawikan. You can do it. Give it all you can," were the heart-lifting cheers of the other animals. As Pawikan got to the finish line, Tamaraw collapsed before he reached the line. Pawikan was declared the winner and crowned the King of the Fields.

Pawikan was treated to a victory banquet by the other animals. From that day on, Tamaraw had great respect for Pawikan. He stayed away from the fields and confined his feeding to the mountainsides and highlands, where he and his kind feed to this day.

Life on Marina Island went back to normal—eating, playing, and sleeping.

---

[5]Onggoy. Ohng `GOH-ee. Monkey

Ibong Adarna
The Enchanted Bird

Once upon a time on the island of Palao there lived a rich old datu.[1] He owned thousands of acres of rice land which produced tons of rice. As a widower, he considered his wealth to be his three handsome sons, who loved him very dearly.

One day the old datu suddenly fell ill. The village shaman couldn't make him well. His magic potions and herbs were of no effect.

By chance, a babaylan[2] was visiting. She diagnosed his illness to be a bad liver. It was caused by a spell cast by a disgruntled diwata[3] who was offended by the datu's failure to offer the yearly gifts of rice cakes at the village temple.

She told the ailing datu that the spell could only be broken by the song of Ibong Adarna,[4] a nightingale that dwelt in the enchanted forest of Mt. Apo. Only its sweet song could restore the datu's health.

The datu could die if the spell was not broken in ten days. There was a grave danger to whoever tried to catch Ibong Adarna. They would run the risk of being turned to stone.

The risk sent a chill to even the bravest of men on the island. None wanted to take the risk. Only the datu's three sons were left to undertake the dangerous task.

The eldest was the first to venture forth. Timbol rode his sturdy horse and took with him a cage and tapa[5] for provision. At the foot of Mt. Apo, he met an old, stooped woodsman sitting cross-legged under a bamboo tree. He was begging for food. Timbol was in a hurry, so he ignored

---

[1]datu. `DAH too
[2]babaylan. Bah `BAH-EE lahn. Medicine woman
[3]diwata. Dee `OO-AH tah. Goddess
[4]Ibong Adarna. Ee BOHNG ah `DAHR nah. A nightingale
[5]tapa. `TAH pah. Dried buffalo meat

the woodsman and passed him by.

Night fell when he reached the enchanted forest. He decided to spend the night under a big majestic lauan tree. At midnight, Timbol was awakened by the sound of flapping wings and the thrashing of branches above him. He looked up to see a marvelous bird. It had a long shimmering tail of gold and silver feathers like a peacock. Its head was crowned with diamonds and pearls. Its breast was covered with golden feathers.

Timbol gasped in wonder. How lucky he was to find Ibong Adarna! He waited until the fabulous bird settled in for the night. To his surprise, the big bird began to sing. Its song was sweet and so melodious that it made Timbol fall asleep. When the bird ended its song, it defecated. The droppings fell on Timbol and his horse. They were turned into stones.

At the datu's mansion, everyone was concerned about the fate of Timbol. Rambang, the second son, left immediately to search for his missing brother.

At the foot of Mt. Apo, he met the same old, stooped woodsman. As did Timbol, he ignored the man's pleas for food. He continued on his mission.

Rambang reached the enchanted forest. That night, while he and his horse slept under the lauan tree, Ibong Adarna came. She sang her sweet song and when she was done, sent her droppings down on Rambang and his horse below. They, too, were turned into stones.

When Rambang failed to return, the datu sent his youngest son, Baruk, to look for his missing brothers and to find Ibong Adarna.

While traveling through their vast rice lands, Baruk came across a farmer and his family who were living in a haystack. Their house had burned and they were weak from hunger. Baruk delayed his trip for two days to help the poor farmer rebuild his hut. Also, he shared his provision of tapa and left some money to tide them over until the next harvest season.

At the foot of Mt. Apo he met the old, stooped woodsman, who begged for food. Touched by his pleas, Baruk shared what little was left of his food. He told the woodsman of his mission to find Ibong Adarna, whose song could break the spell which had been cast on his father.

While Baruk told his story, the old man's appearance changed into smiling, beautiful Diwata, the rice goddess.

Diwata said, "You were the only one who gave me food. You helped the farmer and his family build their hut and gave them money. These acts show that you are a good-hearted man."

The Diwata continued, "I shall give you the things you need so that you will not be turned into stone, and so you can catch and bring Ibong Adarna home." She handed Baruk two small bottles of wine. One bottle he was to drink when he reached the lauan tree. The other one he was to sprinkle on the stones underneath the tree.

Baruk also was given a cape which was to protect him from the deadly droppings of Ibong Adarna.

Diwata then vanished in a cloud of smoke.

Wasting no time, Baruk set out for the lauan tree in the middle of the enchanted forest. He found a spot near the tree, and followed the instructions given by Diwata.

Promptly at midnight, Ibong Adarna appeared. Baruk was dazzled by the bright plumage of the bird who began to sing its sweet and melodious song. The wine kept Baruk wide awake while he enjoyed listening to her song. When Ibong Adarna ceased singing, she sent down a splatter of droppings that fell and slid harmlessly off Baruk's cape.

Baruk hurriedly climbed the tree, grabbed Ibong Adarna, and wrapped her with his cape. Then he sprinkled the contents of the wine bottle on the stones at the foot of the tree. The stones shuddered into life as the missing brothers and their horses.

"Brother! You have rescued us," were the first words that came out of the mouths of the grateful brothers.

With Ibong Adarna securely wrapped in the cape, they raced their swift horses to their home. It was the tenth day. The datu was dying. Adarna was placed in a cage which was hung outside a window of the palace. That night, Adarna sang its sweetest song and the datu was freed from the spell.

With the datu well again, the village people had a fiesta. A fireworks celebration was held in honor of the datu's restored health. The gifts of rice cakes were offered at the village temple for the rice goddess.

In the courtyard of the datu's mansion, a huge lauan tree sprang up where Ibong Adarna lives and sang her nightly songs for the datu and the villagers who lived in peace and good health ever after.

Mt. Mayon
A Monument to Love

In the kingdom of Albay, there lived a beautiful maiden named Malaya,[1] the pride and joy of her father, a datu. She was the answer to the prayers of the proud datu and his wife, the datuin, who fervently prayed for a daughter.

As the years passed, Princess Malaya grew to be the fairest and loveliest maiden in the kingdom. Her beauty was much envied by other girls, and her smiles were ardently sought by love-stricken suitors.

Suitors for her hand came from near and distant kingdoms. They came to the palace bearing gifts of gold necklaces, silk clothes, and delicate porcelain wares. Some were handsome princes and a few were ugly, older ones who were looking for younger wives for their harems. None of them struck a chord of love in Malaya. She enjoyed her independence, for she had a stubborn streak in her veins.

However, one suitor who had not called on Princess Malaya was Wagayon, a young datu from faraway Samar Island. This handsome and dashing prince also loved his freedom. His favorite pastime was sailing his red vinta[2] around the island. When he heard of the beauty and loveliness of Princess Malaya, he set sail for the kingdom of Albay.

He reached the shore of Albay one balmy afternoon. As he approached the beach, he saw the princess swimming as she often did during good weather. Wagayon waved his red kerchief and the princess gaily waved back.

Upon reaching land, Wagayon pulled his vinta to shore and rushed to greet the princess who was waiting for his arrival under a coconut tree. When their eyes met, it was love at first sight. Wagayon was as tall as she

---

[1]Malaya. Mah `LAH EE-AH. Free
[2]vinta. `BEEN tah. Fast sailboat

was petite; rugged as she was graceful. Her pearly white teeth and cheery smile captivated Wagayon. His wavy hair and rippling muscles fascinated Malaya.

They were both so absorbed, breathlessly looking at each other, that they forgot to introduce themselves. Finally, Wagayon broke the silence.

"By the grace of Bathala, beautiful princess, please pardon me a thousand moons for intruding upon your swimming recreation. I'm Prince Wagayon, Datu of faraway Samar. I came uninvited, because I have heard of your beauty and it was my wish to see you in person," said Wagayon, flashing his biggest smile and falling on his knee in a courtly fashion.

Malaya blushed and suppressed an impish giggle. She had never experienced this kind of feeling before. None of her early suitors created as much excitement as this courtly prince brought to her heart.

In response, Malaya said, "Thank you for your kind words, Prince Wagayon. Come with me, please, to our palace and be our guest. I wish to introduce you to my parents, the Datu and Datuin of the kingdom of Albay."

As they walked toward the palace, a hostile man suddenly stepped out of the woods and blocked their path. He brandished his wicked kris.[3] Princess Malaya promptly recognized him as Prince Rabo, one of her rejected suitors. He had been been stalking the princess, and had planned on taking her by force to be his wife.

The appearance of Wagayon thwarted his evil plan. Now he had to kill Wagayon before he could take the princess. Wagayon drew his own kris to defend himself and the princess. The sound of clashing steel blades drew the attention of the villagers. Soon a crowd gathered around the combatants to watch a duel to death. Wagayon was the victor. Prince Rabo lay dead at his feet.

The Datu was grateful to Wagayon for saving his daughter. A banquet was held in his honor. The guests knew at once that the princess was in love. They saw the sparkle in her eyes.

Prince Wagayon rose from his seat of honor to propose a toast. "I would like to toast the beautiful princess Malaya who has so kindly invit-

---

[3]kris. `KREES. Long sword with serpentine blade

ed me to your splendid palace. I also thank the Datu for this wonderful banquet. And now I request the privilege of the hand of the princess in marriage."

A roar of "mabuhay"[4] erupted from the guests and villagers. Princess Malaya was blushing profusely. The datu, who had long wanted to have a son-in-law, raised his glass and in response said, "So be it."

A wedding date was arranged and Wagayon set sail to his island to prepare his people for the coming event.

On the high seas, pirates attacked Wagayon and demanded his money, but he had none to give. Since he was only one against so many, he escaped by plunging into the sea. His abilities as a good swimmer and deep diver saved him from death and he was able to swim safely to his beloved island.

In a few days, word reached Wagayon that the kingdom of Albay had been invaded by pirates, led by Datu Buhawi, another spurned suitor, who was a cruel man. Malaya had turned him down earlier because she did not want to be a member of his harem. He had come to Albay with his pirates to get Malaya. During the battle, the datu and the datuin fled for their lives. Princess Malaya was forcibly carried away by Datu Buhawi to his island kingdom.

Wagayon lost no time setting sail in five massive barangays[5] filled with his fiercest warriors for the pirate island. They landed at dawn and caught Datu Buhawi and his men by surprise. By midmorning, Wagayon and his men had slaughtered the pirates, except for the pirate lord Buhawi and a bodyguard who managed to escape.

Princess Malaya was rescued and the two lovers were happily reunited.

"Be not dismayed, my beautiful princess, the hard days are over," Prince Wagayon reassured her. They set sail for the island of Samar where preparations for the wedding began.

The palace was gaily decorated and the finest china was brought out. The friendly datus of neighboring islands were invited.

Under a canopy of coconut palms, the high shaman performed the

---

[4]mabuhay. Mah `BOO hah-ee. Hurrah, long live
[5]barangay. Bah `RAHN Gah-ee. Huge war boat

wedding ceremony. Fish, deer and buffalo meat were served. Rice and coconut wine enlivened the feast. Fireworks burst in celebration of the happy event. The lovers finally realized their dream of being together for life.

Unknown to the villagers, a stranger disguised as a merchant showed up at the wedding ceremony. Nobody recognized him as the treacherous pirate Buhawi who came to seek revenge for his bitter defeat.

As the newlyweds passed by his side, he drew his dagger and fatally stabbed Wagayon. He fell lifeless to the ground at the feet of the horrified princess.

Upon seeing her beloved husband dead, Princess Malaya seized the dagger and plunged it into her chest. The lovers lay dead, side by side on the ground. Buhawi tried to flee but was caught by Wagayon's men and slain. The tragedy threw the kingdom into total shock.

The bodies of the lovers were brought to the kingdom of Albay, where the beloved princess had spent her life. Hundreds of her people paid their respects to them. The womenfolk sobbed and mourned their great losses. A prominent hillock was chosen for the burial site, where they were laid side by side.

That night, Bathala sent rumblings like the sound of a hundred thunderclaps coming from the sky. This was followed by tremors that shook the earth. Villagers were frightened by the sound and shaking of the ground all around.

Overnight, the hillock became a towering cone-shaped mountain. Pillars of white clouds were seen coming out of the top. In the early morning calm, villagers watched in wonder as the clouds turned into silhouettes of Princess Malaya and Prince Wagayon.

They named the new mountain Mayon in honor of their dearly loved Malaya and Wagayon. On clear days, their dancing silhouettes appear to remind the people of the beauteous Malaya and the noble Wagayon. And so it is today that Mt. Mayon stands in magnificent vigilance over a land where the promise of true love still prevails.

The Hawk and the Hen

Once upon a time on the island of Luzon, an enormous hawk named Kali[1] was soaring majestically with the wind, looking for some mice. From high up in the clouds he espied Manok[2] instead, a good-looking hen. Since he was lonely, he decided to court this adorable chicken.

Manok was busy hunting for food among the bushes when Kali swooped down to her side.

"Good morning, Manok. You're as beautiful as the morning. Pray tell me, what are you doing in this thicket?" Kali asked.

"Oh, good morning to you, too, Kali. I'm just scrounging for some fat, tasty grubs among these bushes," Manok replied.

"I know of a place where there are plenty of juicy grubs. I'd be happy to take you there. Would you like to go with me?" Kali asked politely.

Manok responded coyly, "I'd love to, but I don't have great and mighty wings such as yours to fly along with you."

"Then while you are growing your wings, will you be my sweetheart?" Kali boldly proposed.

"I'd be happy to be your sweetheart," Manok answered, accepting the proposal with a smile.

"You make me very happy, my sweet chicken, to be considered your sweetheart. As a token of our commitment, I wish to give you this gold ring. Please wear it with pride," Kali said. Then he flew away to his aerie on the mountain.

Manok wore the ring on her middle claw and proudly paraded around the flock with her cherished possession.

However, there was one unhappy member of the flock: Tandang.[3] He had also been eyeing Manok and was indeed very jealous.

---

[1]Kali. Kah 'LEE. Hawk
[2]Manok. Mah 'NOOK. Hen
[3]Tandang. Tahn 'DAHNG. Chief rooster

"Do you remember that you promised to be my wife? he asked. "I forbid you to wear that ring. Throw it away!" Fearing that Tandang would make her life miserable, Manok threw the ring away in the bushes.

Not long after, Kali came for a visit. He brought a basketful of tasty grubs as a gift to Manok. When she saw him coming, she fled and hid among the haystacks. Kali searched until he found her and asked her what was wrong.

When Kali noticed that the ring was missing from her middle claw, he was greatly troubled. He asked for an explanation.

"Oh, Kali, I'm very sorry. Yesterday, when I was out in the forest, I saw an ugly snake. I was so frightened by her fangs that I ran away as fast as I could, and I dropped the ring. I tried to find it but I couldn't. Please forgive me," Manok said with her head bowed.

However, Kali was not fooled. He could see by Manok's eyes that she was telling a lie.

"I'm sorry, but I cannot accept your explanation. I'm deeply disappointed that you failed to guard the symbol of our commitment. I will still honor my proposal, but you have to find the ring. While you are looking for it, I'll have to take one of your chicks whenever I find one astray," Kali told her with firmness. Then he flew away.

Manok was in a panic. She asked the flock to help her find the ring. To find the ring, they would need to scratch every nook and cranny on the surface of the earth. And so it is today that chickens are still scratching the ground, looking for the lost ring.

Whenever Kali comes around to collect a chick, Big Rooster sounds the alarm—*Kak-ka-ka-ook*—which warns chicks to run for cover under their mother's protective wings. Even now, Kali is always on the lookout for any stray chicks as the price for the lost ring.

Magno and the Magic Jar

On the island of Cebu there lived a poor boy named Magno. His farmer father had died of a mysterious illness. This sad event left Magno and his mother in very drastic straits.

When they had eaten their last cup of rice, Magno told his mother that he was going to the big city to find work and seek his fortune. Like many poor farm boys, he left for the big city with his mother's blessings.

He went to the marketplace where he asked the merchants for work as a carrier, errand boy, or kitchen helper. Only one, a crafty man with a secret plan in mind, offered him a job.

Magno was hired as a store sweeper. His job was to keep the place clean and the floor shiny. Meanwhile, the merchant led Magno to believe that his late father was the merchant's long lost brother, and he was happy to help a relative.

Magno sent news to his mother that he had found an uncle. She was puzzled, for she had never heard that her dead husband had a brother. When she visited the merchant, she was treated with the utmost kindness. She was given gifts of colorful sarongs and sweet ham to take home. The mother soon forgot all of her misgivings about the merchant's story.

As the widow was preparing to leave, the merchant asked her permission to take Magno with him on a long business trip to another island. She granted her permission. Magno was delighted. This could be the opportunity he was seeking.

Magno and his so-called uncle sailed on a boat and reached the other island without any mishap. From the port, the two traveled by foot toward a huge mountain. Magno got very tired on the way because they didn't have any food. He asked if he could rest and find something to eat.

In a hurry to reach his destination, the uncle told Magno to forget about rest and food. He was rather harsh with his words. The uncle's attitude had sharply changed, and to make his change of attitude clear, he struck Magno with his cane to urge him to go on.

When they reached a cave at nightfall, Magno collapsed in sheer exhaustion. In the morning, his uncle told him about the cave and showed Magno a piece of black coral (a magic stick) which, when rapped on the side of the cave, would open a door.

The uncle further instructed Magno that inside the cave, he would find pots of gold nuggets, diamond earrings, and rings. These things he should not touch, or else he would be turned to stone.

He was to look for a small porcelain tapayan[1]. He was to hand this jar to his uncle at the door of the cave. With the black coral wand, Magno rapped on the side of the cave and a door opened instantly. Inside the cave, he groped his way through eerie twilight. He could see sparkling items scattered around, which were the pots of gold nuggets, diamond earrings, and rings.

He was tempted to take just one diamond ring which he thought would fetch a hefty sum at the market, but his fear of being turned to stone kept his hands at his sides. He found the small porcelain jar among a pile of earthen pots in the rear of the cave.

With the jar safely tucked under his arm, he rushed to the door. The door was ajar. The uncle, who was waiting outside, told Magno to hand him the black coral magic stick first and then the porcelain jar.

Magno handed over the magic stick, but refused to give him the porcelain jar. He sensed that the jar must be of great value, so he decided to hold on to it. The uncle promised him anything he wanted if he would just hand over the jar, but Magno remembered how harshly he had been treated and so turned a deaf ear. The uncle departed angrily, leaving Magno inside the cave with the door closed.

Magno sat down dejectedly beside the door and pondered how to get out of the cave. While holding the porcelain jar, he accidentally rubbed its top. Suddenly, a white plume of smoke popped out. The smoke took the form of a kapre[2], a smiling giant with bulging eyes, fearsome to behold.

Magno cowered in fear and waited to be devoured by this apparition. As a boy, he had heard of evil kapres that swallowed little boys who

---

[1]tapayan. Tah ʿPAH-ee ahn. Ceramic jar
[2]kapre. Kah ʿPREE. A giant ogre

wandered in their realm. Surely he must be in the realm of a kapre.

However, the kapre spoke gently to him. "Magno, do not be afraid of me. I am Sabu, the spirit who has lived inside that jar you hold. By rubbing the top of that jar, you have just released me from an imprisonment of a thousand years. Now you have power over me. In payment for my liberty, I will grant you three wishes for whatever you desire."

Upon hearing Sabu's reassuring words and promise, Magno recovered from his fright. His first wish was to see his mother. In the wink of an eye, Magno was home, reunited with his mother who had been grief-stricken by his disappearance.

Magno showed his mother the magic jar and told her about Sabu, the spirit who could do marvelous things for them. Since they were hungry, Magno's second wish was to have a table full of sweet ham, sausages, roast chicken, mangos, avocados, bananas, and their favorite dessert, bibingka[3]. Sabu made them all appear in the twinkling of an eye and they feasted like kings.

Magno and his mother ate for many days on the leftovers of that bountiful meal. Then Magno made his third and last wish. He asked for the pots of gold nuggets, diamond earrings, and rings from the cave. Sabu's magic power produced the treasure, and immediately he was free from the curse that had imprisoned him.

They sold the jewelry in the market and it brought them large sums of money. They used the money to build a palatial mansion and buy many hectares of rice land and fruit orchards. They shared their riches with friends and relatives.

Magno grew up to be a handsome man and became a sought-after bachelor by the island beauties. He chose the daughter of the datu of the island. A lovely wedding was held. Their children and the people of Cebu worked their land and lived prosperously and happily ever after.

---

[3]Bibingka. Bee `BEENG kah. Rice cake

Dadong
The Cockfighter

On the island of Anda lived a man named Dadong, whose favorite pastime was cockfighting. Often, his rooster would win, but his winnings were too meager to support his wife and daughter. He lost more than he won, so they lived very poorly.

His hut of bamboo and nipa palm was in disrepair. The roof leaked during monsoon season and bone-chilling winds came in through the unrepaired walls, which made the dwelling unbearable.

One day when the season for cockfighting was over, he thought it was time to repair his house, so off to the forest he went to cut some bamboo. He took with him his lunch of boiled rice and dried fish wrapped in a bundle of banana leaves and hung it up on a branch of a tree near where he was to cut bamboo.

When he returned to the tree to get his lunch, the food bundle was missing. Unknown to him, Musang[1] had come and eaten his food. He went home hungry and miserable.

The next day, he went to the forest to cut more bamboo. He brought his usual lunch of boiled rice and dried fish which he again hung on the same tree. Again it disappeared. He went home hungry, sore, and angry.

The third day, he went to the forest again, not to cut bamboo, but this time to catch the thief who had stolen his lunch bundles. He set a trap on his food bundle and hung it on the same tree. Then he hid nearby to wait and watch. Soon Musang appeared and headed straight for the bundle of food. *Bong!* The trap was sprung and the huge cat was caught.

Dadong came out of his hiding place to spear the culprit which had been the cause of his hunger and misery.

Musang begged for mercy: "Oh, Dadong, please spare my life, for I can, and will, be a big help to you." Musang was a forest god who had the

---
[1]Musang. `MOO Sahng. Wild cat

ability to transform himself into other animals.

He brought the cat home on a leash and tied it to a post under the hut. During the night, Musang transformed himself into a fierce gamecock.

The following morning, Dadong was greeted by a loud crowing. Instead of a cat, he found a superb looking rooster tethered to the post.

Dadong was thrilled. He knew he had a winner.

With this gamecock he could go to the sabongan[2] and engage in his favorite pastime. Perhaps he would win big money to keep his wife from nagging him about the lack of food in the household.

At the crack of dawn, he set out for town with the gamecock tucked securely under his arm. On the way, he crossed a river. There he met Buaya,[3] who asked if he could come along with him.

They entered a forest, and met Uhsa[4] who asked if he, too, could join them on the way to the cockpit. The three of them continued their walk until they met Baboy Ramo.[5] Baboy Ramo asked if he could go with them.

Now there were four of them marching to town. As they passed by a big tamarind tree, Onggoy[6] asked if he could go, too. When the party was near the town, Dadong asked his companions what they could do to help him at the cockpit.

Buaya the alligator said that if anyone wanted a contest of diving in the river, he could stay under water longer than any man. Uhsa the deer said that in a contest of speed he could outrun any man. Baboy Ramo the boar claimed that he could beat any man in wrestling. Onggoy the monkey said he could climb a tree faster and higher than any man. Dadong said that he would keep in mind their various skills should a contest occur.

At the cockpit, Dadong entered his gamecock against any and all challengers. To increase his purse he placed a triple bet on his fighter. In the ensuing contests, Dadong's fighter defeated all of his opponents. He used his claws like a cat—which, of course, he really was. The owners of

---

[2]Sabongan. Sah `BOO NGAHN. Town cockpit
[3]Buaya. Boo `OO-AH ee-ah. Crocodile
[4]Uhsa. Oo `SAH. Deer
[5]Baboy Ramo. `BAH boh-ee `RAH MOH. Wild boar
[6]Onggoy. Ohng `GOH-ee. Monkey

50

the defeated cocks were mad at Dadong. They brought more fighters, but Dadong's cock defeated them all.

The other gamblers were not happy. They challenged Dadong to other sports. They brought a man who could stay under water longer than anyone else. Buaya (crocodile) took up the challenge for Dadong. Buaya easily outlasted the man under water. Then they brought out a swift runner and he competed with Uhsa (deer) who also outran the man by a wide margin.

A heavyset, muscular man was brought out for a wrestling contest. Baboy Ramo competed with the giant. The fight went toe to toe, but Baboy Ramo was able to pin the giant.

Finally, they brought a man who boasted he could climb a tree faster and higher than anyone else. Monkey met the challenger and defeated him in the wink of an eye.

The winnings from all of these contests made Dadong a rich man. He brought home ten sacks full of money. It took two horses to carry his winnings. He thanked his friends who had brought him wealth, especially the gamecock, who turned back into a cat and returned to the forest.

With his money, Dadong had a new house built, and had more than enough resources to provide for his family for the rest of their lives.

Dikya
The Jellyfish

There was a time when the sea was ruled by Ballenas.[1] They had a kingdom under the sea. All kinds of fish were their subjects and obeyed the King of Ballenas. All fish had fins, bones, and tails, except for Dikya,[2] who had two stubby legs that were used for walking on land.

One day, Queen Ballena fell ill. The best fish doctors were called to treat the queen's illness, but they were stumped and failed to find the cause of her illness or prescribe a medicine to make her well. In a vision, the queen saw that the cure for her illness was the liver of a monkey.

King Ballena summoned all the fish to the grand palace. The sea boiled with excitement as never before. From the giant manta rays to the lowliest starfish, all came for the greatest assembly in the fish kingdom.

When almost every known fish subject was in the hall, King Ballena announced the reason he had called the assembly. He told them about the queen's mysterious illness, which could not be cured by the best of his physicians. He explained that the queen had dreamed that the liver of a monkey would cure her.

The king asked for volunteers who could bring a monkey to the undersea kingdom. There were no volunteers, for they were fearful of the risks involved. However, the fish were unanimous in their recommendation that Dikya should undertake the mission since he had legs to walk on land.

So Dikya was called by the king to appear at the palace. "You have been chosen by your peers to carry out the mission to bring a live monkey here because you are the only fish with legs. I therefore appoint you to perform this critical task. The queen's health is at stake. You will be well

---

[1]Ballenas. Bah `EE-EH nahs. Whales
[2]Dikya. `DEE kee-ah. Jellyfish

rewarded for a successful job," King Ballena said.

Dikya was apprehensive. He told the king that monkeys do not live in the ocean, and it would be very difficult to convince a monkey to come to the kingdom.

Assuring him, the king said, "Tell Monkey how beautiful life is under the sea and of the abundance of delicious food here. Tell him also how peaceful life is here with no creatures called men to hunt him."

Dikya had some doubts. "Suppose Monkey is still not convinced. Should I bind him with my tentacles and put him to sleep?" Dikya asked.

"Oh, no, no!" the king replied. "Monkey must be brought here alive so I can cut out his liver and grind it into medicine for the queen. Now off with you and use all your persuasive talent to get Monkey to visit our kingdom. Throw in a lot of bananas. That might do the trick."

Although still uncertain of the outcome of his mission, Dikya had to obey the king's order. He surveyed the islands until he found one with plenty of trees. He went ashore quietly and looked around for the monkeys. He found them chattering wildly high up in a tree.

One of them spotted him and came down to look at the funny creature that looked like a fish that walked on two legs.

Dikya greeted the curious monkey. "Good day, Sir Monkey. I am Dikya and I come from the beautiful undersea kingdom of King Ballena. I bring you the good news that the King invites you, as his special guest, to a great festival. There will be plenty of your favorite food and other good things. I assure you that your comfort will be of utmost concern to the king and his staff," Dikya said with all sweetness in his smile.

Now monkeys are adventurous creatures and they like to try new things, so this one thought it would be great fun to visit the undersea kingdom. Dikya offered to let him ride on his back.

When they were far out in the ocean, Monkey asked, "Why is it that the king invited me to be his special guest?" Dikya responded that he had something special which the king wanted as medicine for the mysterious illness of the queen.

Upon hearing this, Monkey thought that it was a bad idea, after all, to accept the invitation. He had a feeling that Dikya had deceived him about the festival, but he kept his thoughts to himself.

On they rode upon the waves. Monkey further inquired about this mysterious illness of the queen that needed his special presence.

Without thinking, Dikya blurted out that the medicine needed was the liver of a live monkey. This revelation sent shivers of cold-blooded fear to Monkey. All of his cunning would be required to save himself from a painful death.

"I would be most honored to donate my liver in order to cure the queen," Monkey said calmly. "However, we have a problem."

"What might be the problem?" Dikya asked as they were getting close to the palace gate.

"Well, to be honest with you, I left my liver hanging on a branch on the tree where we met. I usually carry it with me, but when I'm playing I leave it behind," Monkey sadly confessed.

Dikya was stunned. "Then let's hurry back and fetch it. The king will be very unhappy if we arrive at his palace without your precious liver."

So Dikya made a quick turn around and headed back to the island. The moment they got to the shore, Monkey leaped from his back and raced to the nearest tree. Dikya slowly followed him.

Then it was Monkey's turn to tell the poor jellyfish the truth: his liver was with him all the time and he had made up the alibi to save his skin.

Poor Dikya returned to the palace with a very sad face. When the king heard what had happened, he ordered the guards to flog the jellyfish for his stupidity. The flogging broke all of his bones and his legs. That is why, to this day, all jellyfish have no bones.

As for the queen, she decided to recover without the benefit of a monkey's liver.

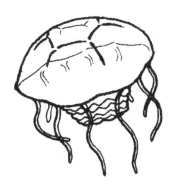

Bindoy
The Greedy Boy

On the island of Negros there lived a widow, Inday, and her son, Bindoy. Their humble hut of coconut leaves and bamboo was at the edge of a lush forest, where many labuyo,[1] deer, and pigs thrived.

Bindoy went hunting every day. Usually he cleaned and cooked his kill in the field, and then ate it all himself, but one day, he brought home a fat red labuyo rooster. His mother was especially pleased, because it had been a long time since there had been any meat for the table.

"This is a fat rooster, Bindoy! We can have a good dinner tonight," said Inday, who was excited about cooking her famous tinola[2] and eating chicken.

As she prepared the chicken, its sweet aroma spread throughout the house. When it was cooked, she called Bindoy to dinner.

At the table, Bindoy scooped up most of the best parts of the chicken—legs, breast, wings, liver, gizzard, and even the backbones. The poor hungry mother was left with only the claws and the neck bones. These she mixed with rice and the little bit of broth left in the pot. She ate her food in painful silence as she watched her greedy son devour his food like a starving pig.

"That was the best dinner we have ever had, Mother!" Bindoy said, smacking his lips. He massaged his distended belly and then went to sleep.

Inday went to bed with a plan to teach her son a lesson. The next day, without waking Bindoy, she left the house very early. She was going to the hills to gather some bananas. On her way, she found a family mourning over a son who had been dead three days. Then, further along

---

[1]labuyo. Lah `BOO ee-oh. Wild chicken
[2]tinola. Tee `NOH Lah. A chicken stew

the way she found another family mourning the loss of a father who had been dead five days.

A little further on, she came across a funeral party which was mourning a woman who died in childbirth. The body was in an advanced state of decomposition. The mourners had their noses covered due to the foul odor coming from the body.

Inday offered to buy the corpse from the family of the deceased. They were glad to have someone take care of the body. She dragged the corpse onto a cart and hid it in the rice granary behind their hut. To keep the odor down, she covered the corpse carefully with plenty of straw.

She arrived home in time to fix dinner. Bindoy was awake and waiting for her. When he saw her climb up the stairs, he called, "What's for supper, Mother? I'm hungry!"

"I brought some bananas from the mountain, but you have to clean them of bugs and dust. They are in the rice granary. Please go and get them." Inday said. Then she went to the kitchen to wash her hands.

As directed, Bindoy went to the rice granary. When he opened the door, the dead woman (who was an aswang[3]) sprang to life. She grabbed Bindoy by the neck and started chewing on his arms. Bindoy let out a blood-curdling yell.

"Mother, come help me. There is an aswang here that is chewing my arms. Please, mother, help me." Bindoy yelled as the aswang sucked his blood. Inday rushed to the rice granary but it was too late. Bindoy had already been devoured. Only his bones remained on the floor.

At midnight, Inday was visited by the aswang. She told Inday that her son could be brought back to life by bringing the bones to the river at dusk. She should dip the bones seven times in the flowing water. Then the aswang flew away, screeching, "Kakak! Kakak!"

The following day, she took the bones to the river at dusk and performed the rite of dipping the bones seven times in the flowing water. The bones assembled themselves into a human body. It was Bindoy. He came back to life. He was weeping with joy when he saw his mother.

"Mother," he said, "I shall always share with you whatever I bring home from my hunt. And I shall never, never be greedy again."

Mother and son were reconciled in happiness and promised to love each other ever after.

---

[3] aswang. Ahs `OO-AHNG. Vampire

Paraluman
The Star Maidens

Once upon a time in the northern mountains of Luzon Island, Tanyag, a handsome youth of the Bontoc tribe, was out inspecting the rice terraces that his family owned. The rice plants were growing fast and in another full moon they would start harvesting the golden grain. Following the harvest, his family would provide the bindian[1] in honor of Lumauig,[2] the supreme god who blesses the rice fields.

It was past midnight when he was on his way home. The full moon cast an eerie radiance as he slowly wended his way through the rice paddies. As he rounded the bend that runs alongside a brook, he caught the sound of laughter. He crept toward the source and saw in the crystal-clear running water seven maidens bathing and frolicking in joyful abandon. They were splashing each other and sending out peals of laughter which mixed with the sound of the bubbling waters.

Tanyag wondered why these village girls were still out at this late hour when they should be at home safely sleeping in their ulog.[3] He crept closer to the bank to have a better view of the maidens. The lovely girls had long, raven-black hair, fair skin, and bodies that glistened in the moonlight. Fairies! Tanyag thought. A cold shiver raced through his body.

Never before had he seen such a sight! The maidens soon came out of the water and headed towards a clump of trees. To Tanyag's amazement, he saw the seven maidens rise above the trees in a line formation. They had wings! They flew out of his sight, leaving a trail of stardust in the moonlit sky.

He ran to his sleeping quarters and went to bed immediately. He was too excited to share the news with his roommates.

---

[1]bindian. `BEEN dee-ahn. A victory feast
[2]Lumauig. Loo `MAH oo-eeg. Supreme God
[3]ulog. Oo `LOHG. Sleeping quarters for maidens

61

The following morning, he visited his father, the chief of the tribe. He described the previous night's sighting of the seven maidens at the brook. His father was not surprised, since he, too, when he was Tanyag's age, had sighted these maidens in a hidden brook near the rice terraces.

The wise chief told him, "These maidens are paralumans.[4] When they visit the earth, they take off their winged dresses and assume human form."

"The next time you see them, try to catch one of them in her human form for your wife," the father advised Tanyag.

"But, Father, how do you catch them? They are not like dalags[5] that you can catch with a tallakib,"[6] Tanyag countered.

"As I said, they have winged dresses that they hang on pine trees when they are bathing. You should find that tree."

"Then what shall I do?" Tanyag asked, as his interest perked up.

The wily father explained, "When you find one of the winged dresses, take it and hide it in your quiver, then wait until they come out of the water. The one who cannot find her wings is the one you can catch. The first night of the full moon is the time they visit the earth."

Tanyag could hardly wait for the next full moon. Indeed, it was a very long wait for him, for he had already fallen in love with the paralumans. He kept the secret to himself, for fear that his roommates might show up at the brook and scare them away.

At midnight, Tanyag was safely hidden on a small hill above the rustling brook. The moon was in full splendor. Surely this must be the night that the paralumans will appear, Tanyag mused to himself as he waited breathlessly. Suddenly, dazzling lights appeared, accompanied by the sound of fluttering wings in a nearby pine tree. When Tanyag regained composure, he was startled to see seven heads bobbing up and down in the clear stream. They were frolicking and having fun.

The brook was alive with the sound of splashing water and tumbling bodies. Tanyag immediately left his hiding place and headed for the tree on which the paralumans had hung their winged dresses. He found the tree and took one of the winged dresses. The wings were like the gossamer

---

[4]Paralumans. Pah ra `LOO MAHNS. Star maidens
[5]dalags. Dah LAGS. Mudfish
[6]tallakib. Tah `LAH keeb. A bamboo fish trap

wings of a butterfly, pure white, and they felt like delicate silk. They had a heavenly radiance. He folded them very carefully and put them in his quiver, hid behind a bush and waited with a pounding heart.

He heard one of them speak. "Sisters, it's almost daybreak. We have had a lot of fun. Let's go home or we might get some scolding from Father Lumaiug."

The maidens rushed to the tree where they had hung their winged dresses. Each one found her own dress, except Gaygayoma,[7] the youngest. She was sure that she had hung it on a branch, but it was not to be found. She started to cry.

"What's the matter, Gaygayoma?" asked the eldest sister. "Why are you crying?"

"I can't find my wings. I know I hung them on this branch, and now they are gone," Gaygayoma sobbed.

"Sisters, let's help Gaygayoma find her wings," the eldest sister ordered.

They searched every nearby tree but they could not find the wings. Since it was almost dawn, the eldest sister told Gaygayoma, "We'll have to leave you behind, dear sister. Wait for daylight and find your wings, and when you do, fly home immediately. We'll tell Father that you have been delayed."

Poor Gaygayoma watched dejectedly as her sisters flew off and streaked through the sky. They left behind a trail of twinkling stardust on their way to their sky world.

Tanyag came out of his hiding place and discreetly approached the distraught maiden. "Good morning, beautiful maiden," Tanyag calmly greeted Gaygayoma, who was frightened upon seeing a human being.

"Who are you, sir?" asked the trembling Gaygayoma.

"Fear not, heavenly muse. I am Tanyag of the Bontoc tribe. I'm here to help you," Tanyag said in a kindly voice.

Gaygayoma looked at Tanyag. Reassured by his kind words, she spoke. "I'm Gaygayoma from the sky world. I lost my wings here and I need them to fly back to my home. Can you please help me find them?"

Tanyag evaded her plea, and instead responded, "I shall be happy to

---

[7]Gaygayoma. Gah-ee gah `EE-OO MAH

take you to my father's house where you will be well cared for until you can get your wings back."

Gaygayoma meekly accepted his offer. With loving care, Tanyag clothed her with his shirt, then carried the beautiful maiden on his broad shoulders to his father's palatial house. There she was received as a celestial guest and given maids to attend to her needs. She soon forgot her loneliness and, as a result of Tanyag's caring and constant attention, they soon fell in love. The two were joined in matrimony.

A lovely baby girl was born to the couple. Half mortal and half divine, she was called Mutya.[8] She was the apple of her father's eye and the pride and joy of both her parents, who denied her nothing, except that she was never to play with his quiver which hung high from the rafter in the ceiling.

Accustomed to always having her own way, Mutya pestered her mother relentlessly, until finally, in desperation, Gaygayoma ordered the maid to take the quiver down.

Mutya was intrigued by the beautifully etched figures of wild animals on the quiver. Since there were no arrows inside, she thrust in her hand and pulled out something which was similar to delicate silk and shaped like giant butterfly wings.

"Look, Mother!" exclaimed Mutya, as she held out the winged dress and moved around as if she were dancing.

When Gaygayoma saw what Mutya held out, she recognized her long missing winged dress. It had been hidden in the quiver all the time.

She slipped quickly into her wings and, like a butterfly, circled around and hastily bade goodbye to her daughter. She flew off to rejoin her father and her sisters in the sky world.

Gaygayoma told her sisters all that had happened during her long absence. There was much rejoicing in the sky world.

When Tanyag returned home from the rice terraces, he was greeted by a sobbing Mutya. She told him what they had found in the quiver and of her mother's sudden departure to the sky world. Tanyag repented bitterly for the wrong that he had done to Gaygayoma.

On the eve of every full moon, Tanyag returns to the rustling brook

---

[8]Mutya. Moo TEE-AH. Pearl

on the mountainside, hoping to see Gaygayoma and her sisters during their earthly visit. They never returned, however, because Lumauig transformed the seven maidens into a majestic constellation, known today as the Pleiades.

Adventures of Lam-Ang

Once upon a time, there lived a man blessed with supernatural powers in the land of Ilocos on the island of Luzon. His name was Lam-Ang.[1] Even at nine months, he was a robust lad. His arms were huge and strong. His noble father, a brave warrior, had been killed in battle against a hostile tribe. When Lam-Ang grew older, he had a vision of his father's death. He asked permission from his mother to seek his father's killers and avenge his death.

Armed with his kampilan,[2] spear, and shield, the powerful youth went forth on his journey of revenge. He rode on the wings of Mangagaratan[3] to speed him in his search and soon caught up with the hostile tribe in the mountains. Lam-Ang challenged the enemy chieftain to hand-to-hand combat, but the chieftain ordered his warriors to surround Lam-Ang and kill him. Their deadly arrows and spears rained on him, but his magical powers made them fall harmlessly away.

Riding on the wings of the wind, he swept down on his foes like a whirlwind and smote them with mighty strokes of his sword. The killing field overflowed with blood. His father's death was avenged.

He fought many more battles to be rid of all the tribes threatening his village. The battles left so much dirt on his body that he stopped by a river to bathe. A hundred village girls took turns washing his long locks of hair with ashes of burnt rice straw. The muck that came off his body was so thick that it caused the death of fish, shrimps, and crabs in the river. After he was cleansed, a gigantic crocodile suddenly grabbed his powerful legs and tried to drag him to the river bottom. Lam-Ang slew the monster with his sharp sword.

Lam-Ang was a handsome man. Tall like a narra tree, he had curly

---

[1]Lam-Ang. Lahm `AHNG
[2]kampilan. Kahm `PEE Lahn. Long sword
[3]Mangagaratan. Man `GAH GAH rah tahn. Wild Wind

black hair and a cheerful smile for everyone. He was much admired and the object of many fanciful glances from pretty maidens in his village. However, Lam-Ang paid little attention to them because his heart was set for Kanoyan, the most beautiful daughter of the richest chief in the village of Kalanutian. He was determined to visit Kalanutian to court this gorgeous lady. On this romantic journey, he brought along his three pets—a white rooster, a yellow-legged hen, and a spotted dog.

On the way, he met Sumarang, a jealous suitor of Kanoyan, who tried to discourage him from his quest for her hand. Since Lam-Ang's heart was so set on Kanoyan, he was undaunted. A duel ensued. Sumarang hurled his spear at Lam-Ang who caught it as if he were picking leaves. He hurled it back at Sumarang, and the force of the blow sent Sumarang's lifeless body hurtling nine hills away.

On his journey he had to pass through the domain of Saridandan, a temptress, with beguiling eyes and charming manners. Upon seeing the brave man, she invited him to stop at her sumptuous home and enjoy the warmth of her bed. Lam-Ang's heart was only for Kanoyan, so he politely turned her down. Saridandan was so frustrated that she vowed she'd never marry.

Lam-Ang arrived at Kalanutian to find the house of Kanoyan crowded inside and out with richly dressed suitors. All were jostling for Kanoyan's attention. How could he get through the rabble of suitors and catch the eye of lovely Kanoyan? He brought out his white rooster and commanded him to flap his broad wings. The thunderous sound caused the collapse of a nearby rice granary. The ear-splitting crash jolted Kanoyan and brought her to the window. She saw the good-looking Lam-Ang. When their eyes met, they were smitten with love. He called his spotted dog to give a roaring howl which instantly restored the rice granary.

The attention-getting deeds of Lam-Ang so impressed the rich parents of Kanoyan that they invited him to dinner. They asked Lam-Ang what his intentions were. He told them of his great love for Kanoyan, and asked for her hand in marriage. The father, however, was not convinced with Lam-Ang's ability to support his daughter. He advised Lam-Ang to return home and bring back his mother because it was the custom to discuss wedding proposals with the future in-laws.

Lam-Ang returned with his mother on a ship loaded with gold earrings, necklaces, and dresses, as well as many more fine gifts. Kanoyan's parents were pleased with the wealth of Lam-Ang.

The wedding of Lam-Ang and Kanoyan was the biggest event that had ever taken place in Kalanutian. Feasting and revelry went on for seven days. Many water buffalo, pigs, and waterfowl were butchered to feed the thousands of guests. The couple had a very happy wedding.

Before they could settle down in Kalanutian, the village chief told Lam-Ang that it was his turn to catch Rarang,[4] a giant lobster, which was devouring fish, crabs, and shrimps. Without seafood, the village might starve. Many brave men had already perished in their attempts to destroy Rarang.

Before he undertook the dangerous task, Lam-Ang confided to Kanoyan about a dream in which he saw his impending death. He saw himself being swallowed by Berkakan,[5] a monstrous white shark. He warned his wife that she'd know he was dead if the stairs danced, the kitchen roof fell, and the stove broke to pieces.

He went looking for Rarang, which he destroyed with his mighty sword. But as he foretold, Lam-Ang was swallowed alive by Berkakan as he swam toward shore. All of the signs that he told his wife about occurred.

However, Kanoyan was not sorrowful, for Lam-Ang had also revealed to her how he could be brought back to life. She was to wait for instructions from his pet rooster, who would advise her what to do. After the monstrous shark swallowed him, his bones were excreted three days later. Upon the directions of the rooster, Kanoyan sent divers to gather the bones of Lam-Ang in the bottom of the sea. These were delivered to Kanoyan, who wrapped them in her tapis.[6] Then she called the three magical pets together. At her command, they made a thunderous noise heard throughout the village. The rooster crowed, the hen flapped her wings, and the dog howled. Lam-Ang was brought back to life and rejoined his wife.

They returned to their home with great joy and lived happily ever after.

---

[4]Rarang. Rah `RAHNG. Giant lobster
[5]Berkakan. Behr `KAH kahn. White shark
[6]Tapis. TAH Pees. Long skirt

Mariang Makiling
The Benevolent Lady of the Mountains

Once upon a time, there lived in the cloud-kissed mountains of Laguna a tall and graceful woman named Mariang Makiling.[1] She was half goddess and half human, for her father was a woodland god and her mother was a lovely maiden named Filipinas.

It is said that when she was born, the moonbeams were at their brightest, and she was serenaded by the soft murmur of waves from a near-by lake.

Her mother was taken to the sky world after Mariang Makiling was born, so she was tended by the nymphs in the forest. As she grew, she acquired the divine nature of her father, which enabled her to change herself into an animal of the forest or a human being. In her human form she had big brown eyes, long and abundant hair, and a clear brown complexion. Her hands and feet were smooth and delicate because she had never tilled the soil.

Lovely as she was, she was also enigmatic. An old woman who lived at the foot of the mountain said that she had seen Mariang Makiling once from a distance. She saw her passing over the talahib[2] so lightly and airily that she did not even make its delicate blades bend. Also, a hunter had seen her at dusk, sitting motionless on the edge of a precipice, letting her hair float in the wind.

Mariang Makiling was much loved and adored by the mountain folks. As a demi-goddess, she could make herself visible or invisible. Folks say that her favorite time for appearing was after a storm. Then she could be seen as a blue mist drifting at dusk over fields and orchards. Folks knew that she had been around when they saw their devastated rice fields

---

[1]Mariang Makiling. Mah `REE AHNG Mah `KEE leeng
[2]talahib. Tah `LAH Heeb. Reed grass

restored to life, broken fruit trees standing upright, and when scattered farm animals found their way home. Rivers and streams went back to their normal levels.

When poor mountain folks celebrated a baptism or a wedding, Mariang Makiling would lend them the clothing or jewels needed for the occasion. She had one condition — that they return them and give her a pullet, white as milk — one that had never laid an egg.

When Mariang Makiling was in a charitable mood, she would go around the mountain villages in the guise of a simple country maid. Village women who went to the mountains for firewood and wild berries say that they sometimes met this simple country maid on the way home. When they untied their bundles of firewood and opened their baskets, they would find a gold coin or a pair of gold earrings.

One popular story about Mariang Makiling involved a hunter who was in pursuit of a wounded wild boar. The hunter saw the animal hide in a hut deep in the forest. When he got to the door, a beautiful woman with hair that reached the floor appeared and smilingly greeted the hunter:

"The wild boar belongs to me and that's why it came here to hide in my hut. You are welcome to rest here and eat before you go home. Please come in."

The bewildered hunter was speechless and did as he was told. He was served roast venison, rice, and mangoes, which he ate without a single word. Mariang Makiling, in the custom of the mountain folks, kept filling his plate with food. It was also the custom that the host usually provided the guest with some food to take home to the family.

The gracious host told her guest, "Please take these yams with you and give them to your wife. They are very good. I raised them in my garden." Mariang Makiling handed a sack of yams to the hunter which he placed in his backpack.

On the way home, the backpack seemed to weigh heavier with each passing hour, so he took out some of the yams and threw them away. When he got home, his wife opened his backpack and to her surprise found golden coins. The hunter regretted throwing away some of the yams. He realized now that the lady he had met in the mountains was the fabled Mariang Makiling.

While Mariang Makiling could be extravagantly generous with her gifts, she could also be swift in punishing those who were selfish and stingy.

Mountain folks tell a story of two hunters who were on their way home, carrying a wild boar and a deer that they had killed. They happened to meet an old woman who begged for some of the meat. The hunters told her that they had a big family to feed, and left the poor old woman crying in hunger.

Soon after, as they descended to the lowlands, they heard a loud, frightening sound behind them. The sound was like a thundering herd of water buffalo. The hunters, fearing a stampede, threw down their burdens and climbed the nearest tree. Their hunting dogs fled in terror with their tails tucked between their legs. From their perch the hunters saw a rolling cloud of dust in the form of a snorting buffalo that devoured their kills.

Mariang Makiling at times exhibited the tender part of her human side. A story is told about her love for Dimas, a young farmer who farmed the mountain slopes. Dimas supported his infirm parents with the produce of the farm—succulent lanzones, sweet rice, and fat cattle. His fellow farmers could not match the quality of the produce that Dimas sold. Often his farm was spared from the yearly torrential rains and typhoons which ruin farm and orchard lands. As a result, he was able to sell farm produce when his fellow farmers had none. They suspected that Dimas was protected by an invisible spirit.

When he reached the conscription age of 21, when every young man was required to serve in the dreaded army, Dimas' aged parents were worried that their sole support would be gone. To prevent this from happening they arranged his marriage to a farmer's daughter, who lived on the other side of the mountain.

On the eve of the wedding day, on his way to his future wife's village, Dimas met a young woman who suddenly appeared on the road. The woman was unusually beautiful. Her smiling face showed pearly white teeth. Her jet black hair, which almost reached the ground, was flowing enchantingly in the light breeze.

Dimas was startled but unafraid. He had heard of Mariang Makiling and had been wanting to meet her. In a sweet tone mixed with sorrow and compassion, she said, "I have been your guardian for all those disastrous years when you were able to grow fruits and rice and raise cattle on your land. I have loved you because I've seen that you are good and industrious. I had hoped that you would recognize my love and kindness and therefore devote your life to me. But I see you need the companionship of an earthly woman. I have come to give you my gift for your bride."

Mariang Makiling handed Dimas a bundle containing a wedding gown, a golden ring, and a chain necklace. Before Dimas could thank her, Mariang Makiling disappeared in a blue mist. She didn't even ask for her customary white pullet in return. Sadly, he took the gift to his bride. However, his bride refused to wear the bridal gown and the jewels on their wedding day.

This refusal deeply hurt Mariang Makiling. She, who had been generous with gifts for the mountain folks on special occasions, took offense. After that time, Dimas had to scramble for a living. To this day, Mariang Makiling has not shown herself to the mountain folks of Laguna. However, the legend of her many good deeds and mystical kindnesses continues to be told and retold by the mountain people.

Magbangal
The Rice Planter

Once upon a time, there was a man named Magbangal,[1] who lived in a mountainous region of Bukidnon on the island of Mindanao. One bright morning, he sat on the stairway of his hut and pondered where to plant the rice seeds brought to him by the rice birds from another island.

The rice birds told him, "Plant these rice seeds in the mountains where there is plenty of sun and water. When they bear the grains, you and your family will have plenty of food and we, too, will have some."

He knew of a place in the mountains where the sun shone most of the day and a spring was nearby, so he called his wife.

"Masikla, tomorrow I shall go to the mountains to clear land for the rice seeds. Please prepare my food, for I shall be away the whole day," Magbangal said.

"May I go with you and help you clear the land?" Masikla begged, since she had nothing to do in their hut except to weave the rough tapa cloth.

Magbangal sternly denied Masikla's request. "No, Masikla, you cannot come with me. Keep yourself busy with your loom, for we will need clothes to keep us warm this coming rainy season."

The following morning, Magbangal prepared his tools. He brought with him ten axes and ten bolos, a sharpening stone, and a bamboo tube for water. He also had his food of rice and fish wrapped in banana leaves.

He found the place in the mountains and started cutting the trees. The first tree was made into a bench on which Magbangal stretched out to rest. Then he ordered his axes and bolos to carry on with the work of clearing the planting area.

"Axes and bolos, sharpen yourselves with the sharpening stone and proceed to cut the trees and clear the land."

---

[1]Magbangal. Mahg Bah 'NGAHL

77

The tools did as they were told, for they were possessed with magic. Magbangal had obtained these tools from the Ancient One who lived in a secret cave of Mt. Matutum.

He had met the Ancient One when he was hunting and shared with him the meat of a deer he had killed. In appreciation, the Ancient One gave him ten axes and ten bolos, which he was told possessed magical powers to do his bidding.

From his bench, Magbangal watched the axes and bolos clear the land while he ate his rice and fish, and played on his bamboo flute. By nightfall, a good portion of the land had been cleared.

Masikla happily greeted him and had his supper ready. The following day he told Masikla that he had to go back to the mountains to clear more land. He took with him his ten magic axes and bolos.

He told Masikla to stay at home and finish her weaving. However, Masikla was bored with her weaving, so she secretly followed Magbangal to the mountains.

From a distance, Masikla heard trees being chopped down. She thought that her husband must have some help, for he had ten axes and bolos which he couldn't use all at the same time. The thunder of many falling trees indicated that all the tools were being used.

When Masikla got to the kaingin,[2] she saw Magbangal under the shade of a pine tree. He was sitting comfortably on a bench and playing his bamboo flute. From her hiding place behind a big pine tree, she could also see that the axes and bolos were cutting down brushes and trees without anyone wielding them. Amazing! Masikla thought. So that is how Magbangal was able to clear land for the rice plants. She hadn't known that Magbangal had some secret power to command the tools to cut by themselves.

Suddenly, the tools ceased cutting and Magbangal dropped his flute and jumped to his feet. He grabbed one of the bolos and it cut off his little finger. As if he were in a trance, he woke up and exclaimed, "Somebody is watching me, for the bolo cut my finger off!"

Masikla stepped out of her hiding place and ran to her husband. "Oh, Masikla!" he cried. "You caused all of this trouble. If only you hadn't

---

[2]kaingin. Kah EEN NGEEN. A clearing in the mountain for planting rice

78

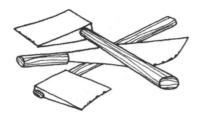

followed me and learned the secret of my axes and bolos, we would have been freed from working with our own hands and saved from the labor of planting rice. From here on we will always be clearing the land and planting rice with our bare hands."

Since then, Magbangal and his descendants have been planting and harvesting rice manually. And so it is today that planting rice is hard work. Planters are bent from morn 'til the set of sun.

Trial at Mt. Pinatubo

Once upon a time there was a very old hermit named Sinukuan,[1] who lived in the thick forest of Mt. Pinatubo on the island of Luzon. He had left for the forest many, many moons before to seek shelter from the abuse of his neighbors who were jealous of his intelligence. The gods had given him the power of wisdom which he used to help people solve their problems. This made him very popular among the villagers.

The shamans were unhappy because many villagers would rather see Sinukuan for advice about their health and their problems, so they organized the village people to drive Sinukuan out of the village. That is what caused Sinukuan to seek refuge in the thick forest of Mt. Pinatubo where he chose to live with animals rather than human beings.

He used his wisdom to live with animals. In time, the wild animals and other life forms accepted Sinukuan as one of them. He learned the language of the animals and birds and was able to talk to them. Even in his human form, the animals feared him not, for Sinukuan had earned their trust and respect. He became their friend, judge, and guardian.

One day a doe came to him to settle a dispute she had with a boar. "Oh, Wise One," the doe said, "this boar has been disturbing me all night with his grunts and groans so that I have not been able to sleep well. And now, because of lack of sleep, I'm too thin and my mate the stag refuses to help me start a family. It's all the boar's fault."

Sinukuan summoned the boar to hear his side of the story.

"Oh, Sinukuan," the boar explained, "I have to grunt and groan every night because my mate has to feed our babies. When they suck her milk, I have to grunt and growl to drive away Python who wants to eat our babies."

Sinukuan ruled that Boar was not at fault for disturbing the sleep of

---

[1]Sinukuan. See `NOO KOO Ahn

81

Doe since he had to protect the babies from Python.

Python was then called to explain why he was always threatening to snatch the babies of Boar.

"Oh, Wise One," Python said, "I live by myself and eat only once in a blue moon. Whenever I look for food at night, I look for any animal that is asleep, but often I cannot find one because the monkeys have been driving them away. I live in constant fear of starvation. The monkeys are to blame for all this mess."

Sinukuan decreed that Python was not at fault for looking for something to eat at night. So he called the monkeys to explain why they were the cause of Python's food problem.

"Oh, Wise One," the monkey said, "we are not to blame for Python's hunger. We are always on the move from tree to tree at night to get away from Mosquito, who keeps on stabbing us with his sharp dagger of a tongue and sucking away our blood."

Sinukuan was beginning to get to the bottom of this mess in the forest. Next to be consulted was Mosquito.

"Mosquito, you have been charged with stabbing the monkeys with your sharp dagger of a tongue and sucking their life blood away. What do you say to that?"

But Mosquito was so bloated with blood that he was in a stupor and couldn't defend himself against the charges.

Sinukuan, therefore, sentenced Mosquito to three days in solitary confinement. During his confinement he lost his voice and his dagger of a tongue was reduced to a needle point.

And so it is today that male mosquitoes make no sound when they bite. Only the females still sing before they sting, which warns the victims to move away.

Legend of the Mango

Once upon a time, there lived in the peaceful village of Kalibo on the island of Panay a man named Dogedog[1] and his wife Mabuot.[2] They were an unlikely pair, for the man's main trait was a violent temper and the woman had a gentle disposition. However, they appeared in the eyes of the villagers to get along well.

Dogedog and Mabuot had a beautiful daughter whose name, Malanga,[3] was synonymous with loveliness. She had a bit of the temper of her father and the good disposition of her mother. These qualities endeared her to the many suitors who sought her hand in marriage.

Dogedog had plans for his daughter. He wanted a son-in-law just like him—a man with a flair for bravado, who was aggressive and who could stand on his own feet in arguments.

One day, Dogedog announced to Malanga that he had found such a man for her. His name was Labaw, son of another wealthy farmer in another village. He set the wedding day for the next harvest moon.

Surprised, and very dismayed at this news, Malanga responded, "Father, I respect your choice of my future husband but, bitter as you might feel about it, I cannot accept him. I have to go by what my heart says. I prefer to marry a man I can love and honor."

Seeing her daughter very unhappy at the decision made by her husband, Mabuot tried to talk to Dogedog about their daughter's wishes. She pleaded for him to reconsider his choice for their daughter's happiness, even though it was a tribal custom for parents to choose their child's spouse.

Mabuot's pleas were to no avail. Dogedog was stubborn and he had made up his mind. Malanga was in deep anguish.

---

[1]Dogedog. Dah `GEE Dog
[2]Mabuot. Mah `BOO OHT
[3]Malanga. Mah 'lahn 'gah

Meanwhile, Labaw went about bragging to the village people that Dogedog had chosen him to be his son-in-law. He spent the days carousing with his friends and getting drunk with tuba[4] every night until the eve of the wedding day.

Since the betrothal was announced, Malanga had secluded herself in her room. For fear of meeting Labaw, she had given up her afternoon pastime of walking with her maids and friends among the coconut trees. Previously, during sunny days she and her entourage loved to visit a nearby batis,[5] where they would spend many happy hours bathing and playing in the crystal waters. Her mother was distressed about the change in Malanga's daily routine. Delicious foods brought to her room were left untouched. Soon she grew wan and weak.

The household of Dogedog made preparations for the big event in the village. Cows, pigs, goats, and chickens were butchered for the feast which would follow the wedding ceremony. The whole village was invited to the wedding. Dogedog was a rich man and owned many acres of rice land.

Unknown to her parents, Malanga slipped quietly out of the house on the eve of her wedding day and went to the spring where she had gathered many happy memories playing with her friends.

On the morning of the wedding, Mabuot went to wake her daughter. "Malanga dear, please come out, for today is your wedding day," Mabuot called as she knocked on her daughter's door. There was no answer, not even stirrings of a person getting ready to open the door. Mabuot called Dogedog and both of them opened the door. Malanga was not in her room. Her bed was neatly made up and showed that she had not slept on it.

At first, Dogedog and Mabuot were not alarmed. They thought their daughter was with her friends, and that she would show up on her wedding day. But as the morning hours passed and there was no sign of Malanga, they began to worry. Servants were sent around to check with her friends and search the village.

---

[4]Tuba. Too 'Bah. Coconut beer
[5]Batis. Bah 'tis. Spring

They found the lifeless body of Malanga beside the spring with a dagger on her side. She had thrust the dagger through her heart. A note clutched in her hand read:

Forgive me, my beloved parents, for taking my life which you gave me. I chose this end, for my heart is only for the man I love.

Dogedog and Mabuot were crazed with grief. The wedding that they had planned had turned into a funeral. Their guests were in mourning, too, because of the sad event.

In the weeks that followed, Dogedog was haunted by a dream. He dreamt that Malanga appeared to him arrayed in her wedding gown. Her face was sorrowful, with tears dropping like beads from her eyes. The dream was so real that Dogedog wanted to reach out for her hands and ask for her forgiveness.

Malanga called to him: "Father, go to the spring by the hills, where you will find a tree laden with golden fruits. Bathala has created this tree to bear fruit as a gift for the sacrifice I made with my heart."

Dogedog and Mabuot went to the spring, and there they found a huge tree with branches full of heart-shaped fruits. The fruit had a yellow skin and had a marvelous scent. They plucked one of the fruits and tasted it. The pulp was sweet and juicy. They had never seen or tasted a fruit of this kind before.

In honor of their daughter who sacrificed her heart for love, they named the fruit Manga.

The fruit tree spread throughout all the islands. And so it is today that when mango is in season, it is the favorite fruit for refreshment. Filipinos call it the queen of fruits in the islands.

About the Authors

NIMFA MATEO RODEHEAVER is on the faculty of Newcomer High School in San Francisco, California, where she also serves as a department head, curriculum writer, and facilitator. Teaching English as a Second Language has been her forte for the past 25 years. She has taught a variety of students with limited proficiency in English by using oral and written tools.

Nimfa obtained her undergraduate and advanced degrees from institutions of higher learning in the Philippines and in the U. S. Her Ph. D. is in Educational Management. She has taught from pre-K to the university level in the past 30 years. She is the author of the well-received textbook *Acquiring Basic Concepts in Science and Language*, which is used in most California public high schools.

In 1991 she was chosen Star Teacher of the Year by her school and was nominated California Teacher of the Year for her staunch commitment to disadvantaged students and her innovative contributions to minority education. From 1991 to 1993, she was a mentor teacher of the San Francisco Unified School District. She is a teacher-consultant for the University of California at Berkeley's Bay Area Writing Project.

ARTEMIO R. GUILLERMO, a former Fulbright-Crusade Scholar, has been on the faculty of Bowling State University, Arkansas State University, and the University of Northern Iowa. He has taught courses in communication, public relations, and journalism. A published author of articles and research papers in refereed journals, he prepared a handbook on learning journalism concepts which was used in *Personalized System of Instruction*. His latest book, *Churches Aflame*, was published by Abingdon Press, Nashville, Tennessee.

Art graduated with a B.A. Degree from Silliman University in the Philippines and obtained his M.A. in Journalism and Ph.D. in Communication from Syracuse University, Syracuse, New York. He also took graduate courses at Medill School of Journalism, Northwestern University in Evanston, Illinois. He lives in Cedar Falls, Iowa.

About the Illustrator

TINA SEVILLA is a Filipino artist who grew up in Chicago, Illinois, and the San Francisco Bay Area. Through her artwork, she expresses her love and appreciation of the Philippine culture. She has created artwork for a Filipino-American magazine, a line of Philippine greeting cards, and other works which portray the warmth of the Filipino people. Tina is a Graphic Design graduate of San Jose State University, and is a freelance illustrator in the Bay Area.